I0658167

STREET KINGS 2

Lock Down Publications and
Ca$h
Presents
Street Kings 2
A Novel by *Hood Rich*

Street Kings 2

Lock Down Publications
P.O. Box 870494
Mesquite, Tx 75187

Visit our website @
www.lockdownpublications.com

Copyright 2019 Hood Rich
Street Kings 2

All rights reserved. No part of this book may be re-
produced in any form or by electronic or mechanical
means, including information storage and retrieval sys-
tems without permission in writing from the publisher,
except by a reviewer who may quote brief passages in
review.
First Edition August 2019
Printed in the United States of America

*This is a work of fiction. Names, characters,
places, and incidents either are products of the au-
thor's imagination or are used fictitiously. Any simi-
larity to actual events or locales or persons, living or
dead, is entirely coincidental.*

Lock Down Publications
**Like our page on Facebook: Lock Down Publi-
cations @**
www.facebook.com/lockdownpublications.ldp
Cover design and layout by: **Dynasty Cover Me**
Book interior design by: **Shawn Walker**
Edited by: **Jill Alicea**

Stay Connected with Us!

Text **LOCKDOWN** to 22828 to stay up-to-date with new releases, sneak peaks, contests and more…

Thank you.

Submission Guideline

Submit the first three chapters of your completed manuscript to ldpsubmissions@gmail.com, subject line: Your book's title. The manuscript must be in a .doc file and sent as an attachment. Document should be in Times New Roman, double spaced and in size 12 font. Also, provide your synopsis and full contact information. If sending multiple submissions, they must each be in a separate email.

Have a story but no way to send it electronically? You can still submit to LDP/Ca$h Presents. Send in the first three chapters, written or typed, of your completed manuscript to:

LDP: Submissions Dept
Po Box 870494
Mesquite, Tx 75187

DO NOT send original manuscript. Must be a duplicate.

Provide your synopsis and a cover letter containing your full contact information.

Thanks for considering LDP and Ca$h Presents.

Hood Rich

Chapter 1

Filipino staggered to his feet. The sunlight felt as if it was baking his forehead. It was ninety degrees outside, hot and extremely humid. The China White and Hennessey was a volatile mix. His eyes were low. His stomach fluttered. His mouth felt drier than a desert.

He struggled to read the text from Fancii once again, which stated that she needed him to get into contact with her again, that it was an emergency, and imperative that he did so. He squeezed his eyelids together and tried as hard as he could to focus on scrolling down his call log. When he came upon her face, he clicked on it. He staggered and placed the phone to his ear. He wondered what the matter could be. He prayed that it was nothing serious. He and Fancii had recently lost their mother to murder. Ever since the event had taken place, Fancii had not spoken a word to him, and the fact that she was contacting him out of the blue was terrifying. He could only think of the worst possible things. "Come on, man. Come on," he spoke into the phone as it worked to connect their calls.

Combo cocked the automatic and smiled under his mask. He watched from a distance as Filipino staggered drunkenly back and forth on his feet, oblivious as to what was about to go down. He pointed at him and alerted the other hittas inside of his van. "Say, there go one of them fuck niggas right there, potna. Roll up slow, and make sure you niggas empty them clips! Y'all got that shit?" he hollered, getting excited. One of his hittas pulled the side door to the van all the way open and got his own Tech Nine ready to blow. Filipino and Noodles were the most wanted men in South Los Angeles. Each man had a fifty thousand dollar apiece bounty on his head, bounties that could be collected whether they were cashed in dead or alive.

Fancii's line seemed to ring and ring. Then her voicemail service came on. Filipino hung up and tried to call her again. Now he was really beginning to panic. "Why would she text me and not pick up?" he said out loud. It made no sense to him. He listened to the line ring some more. It sounded to him as if it was the loudest it had ever been. "Come on, Sis, pick up. Pick up. Pick up. Pick up," he begged, walking along the curb.

The driver of the van waited until he was three houses away before speeding up and slamming on the brakes right in front of Filipino. "Say, potna!" Combo hollered, and then he was squeezing his trigger.

Boom. Boom. Boom. Boom.

Shells hopped out of his weapon and onto the van's floor with smoke coming from them.

The first four bullets slammed into Filipino's chest and knocked him backward. He landed on the sidewalk and struggled to get up. His eyes were bucked. His chest felt like it was on fire. His life flashed before his eyes. The entire world seemed to move in slow motion. He came to his feet and felt three more slugs smack into his back. The impact knocked him forward. He wound up in the grass in a push-up position, struggling to get up as bullets cut at the lawn and spit dirt into the air.

Boom. Boom. Boom.

Combo aimed to kill. He wanted to knock one half of the duo off of the map. He knew what Filipino and Noodles were capable of as a team. If he could kill fifty percent of the team, it would save him a lot of heartache and pain down the road.

A bullet pierced Filipino's right shoulder. It felt like he was being stabbed with a flaming sword. He hollered out in pain and fell back to his stomach. He tried desperately to crawl across the grass.

Noodles jumped from atop Sky. When the shooting had started, he'd thrown her to ground and gotten on top of her to protect her from the barrage of firepower. "Stay yo' ass down!" he demanded. He pulled both Glock Forties from his waistband and ran out the front of the house. From the porch, he spotted the van. He saw that its door was wide open. Three shooters were trying as best they could to kill his right-hand man. Filipino lay on his stomach in the grass, unmoving. There was a puddle of blood surrounding his body. "Bitch niggas."

Bocka. Bocka. Bocka. Bocka. Bocka.

Noodles rushed down the steps and toward the van fearlessly. *Bocka. Bocka. Bocka.*

A bullet slammed into Combo's shoulder. He dropped his weapon. It fell onto the street, and then his entire arm went numb. He could feel the blood rushing into his shirt and down to his pants. "Pull off! Pull off!" he ordered, lying backward on the ground.

Noodles rushed the van.

Bocka. Bocka. Bocka. Bocka. Bocka.

His bullets shattered the side window. When the van door closed, five more of his bullets ricocheted off of it. The van sped down the street and he chased it, busting, splashing the back window. He finger fucked his triggers until his Glocks were clicking in his hands. The street was littered with shells.

"Bitch-ass niggas! I'ma kill you son of a bitches!" he swore. He looked down and saw the Tech Nine that Combo had used in the middle of the street. The clip that hung out of it was as long as a table's leg. He glanced over to Filipino, and once again saw that he was unmoving. He lowered his head and slowly made his way on to the sidewalk and then across the grass. "Damn," he muttered. He knelt beside his body with tears in his eyes. "Say, Cuz, you good?" He turned him over and almost had a heart attack.

Filipino shook. He couldn't stop kicking his legs no matter how hard he tried. His shoulder injury was killing him. It felt like someone was digging a screwdriver into his shoulder and twisting it over and over again. His chest hurt so bad that it went numb. Filipino struggled to talk. He wanted to tell Noodles to get him to a hospital fast, that he could barely breathe. He felt like he was being choked by his own blood. But every time he tried to open his mouth, he felt too weak to do so.

Sky rushed out of the house. She ran over to Noodles. "Nadell, get out of here now! The police on they way!" she advised. She saw the state of Filipino and shook her head. Whoever was after them wasn't playing no games. They were trying to kill him. She would have to move for sure. She wondered how they knew where to locate them. That terrified her. She knelt beside Noodles. "Did you hear me? You gotta get the hell out of here."

Tears ran down Noodles's cheeks. He wiped them away. He could hear the sounds of the paramedics and fire trucks in the background. He stood up. "Sky, when they get here, you make sure they take care of my brother. Make sure you text me right away so I can know what hospital they took him to. That's my nigga right there." He wiped the tears from his face again. "Do you hear me?" he snapped.

She looked over at Filipino. He looked terrible. "Yes, Noodles. Now go!" She pointed toward his car.

Noodles eyed Filipino once again and felt sick to his stomach. "A'ight, man." The sirens got louder and closer. He ran to his car, and just before he got inside, Sky called to him.

"Noodles, thank you again. Thank you for jumping on top of me. I owe you!" she screamed. "Now go!"

Noodles jumped behind the wheel of the car, started it, and stormed away from the scene with both of his Glock Forties on his lap. They were still warm from the shootout. "I'ma kill them niggas. I'ma find out who did this shit, and I'ma kill 'em," he swore.

***

Fancii felt dizzy. She was on her knees inside of Mills's bathroom feeling sicker than she'd ever felt in her entire life. She didn't know what was going on. Her forehead rested on the side of the toilet bowl. The coolness of the porcelain felt good to her.

Mills knocked again. "Fancii, baby, what's going on in there?" he asked with genuine concern and mild irritation.

Fancii shook her head. "I don't know. I don't feel right. Maybe it's something I ate," she offered before spitting into the toilet bowl.

Mills held her phone in his hand. "Well, I got your phone right here, and you have a weird text up on it. I think you should call whoever this is back."

Fancii dry heaved and held her face inside of the toilet. Sweat slid down the side of her forehead and into her ear, tickling her. She wiped it away. "Who is it? What does it say?"

Mills squinted his eyes. "It's a message from some-body named Nadell. He says your brother has been shot up really bad. That he's in the hospital. This person also wants to know where you are." Mills swallowed his spit. He was wondering what the hell he'd gotten himself into by messing with Fancii, the model from Crenshaw.

Fancii's eyes got bucked. She bounced up. Her head felt like it was about to spin off of her neck. She placed out her arms and held her balance by putting her hands on the walls. She waited for the feeling to calm a tad bit, then made her way to the bathroom door and twisted the knob. "Give me the phone." Even through her sickly state, she was able to gather the feelings of irritation for him reading her phone messages. They weren't to-gether, and even if they had been, he was overstepping his boundaries.

Mills handed it to her. "Is there anything I can do to help?" he asked, concerned for her well-being.

Fancii shook her head and closed the door. She di-aled Noodles's cell phone number and sank to the floor. She was out of breath.

It rang twice before Noodles picked up. He wanted to snap. He wanted to curse her out. There were still so many questions circling around her. The last time he'd seen her she'd been rolling away from the church inside of a Range Rover that he was sure was being driven by a dude. Fancii had been the love of his life, and as it stood, he had no idea where they stood amongst each other. "Hello, Fancii?"

"Noodles, I'm here." She took a deep breath and swallowed her spit.

"Man, where the fuck are you? Filipino just got shot a bunch of times. He's in the hospital. I don't know what his condition is, but you need to get the fuck down there so you can let me know what's what."

Fancii covered her mouth with her left hand. The feeling of nausea increasing again. "Noodles. Oh my God, what happened?"

"Man, I don't know. We got caught slipping. You know what it is. We live in L.A. That's neither here nor there though. You need to get yo' ass down to the hospital right now. I'm texting you the information right now. I don't care what you got going on. You get to bro's side. You hear me?" Noodles ordered her.

Fancii was on her knees, bent over. Her forehead planted against the linoleum. Tears ran from her eyes and down her neck. "Not my brother, Noodles. Not my brother. I just lost my mother, Noodles. It's not fair."

Noodles felt a lump form in his throat. A chill went down his spine. He lowered his head and tried his best to not imagine how Filipino looked the last time he saw him. "Look, Fancii, that's my brother. That nigga's a savage. He ain't gon' let a few bullets take him out of the game, you can believe that. Just get down there so you can keep me in tune with everything that goes down with him. Please."

Fancii nodded her head as if he could see her. "Okay, Noodles. I got you."

"Good. Be careful, baby, and remember to keep me in tune every step of the way. I'ma be waiting patiently by my phone, a'ight?"

Fancii nodded again. She couldn't believe something like this was happening in such a short span of time. Life seemed as if it was closing in in her. She felt so alone, and if Filipino didn't make it, it would become official. She would have no one. "Noodles, I love you, baby. Do you hear me? I love you with all of my heart."

Noodles wiped away his tears of anger. He had murder on his mind. He didn't care if he was alone. He was going to holler at Combo and his crew all by himself. "I love you too, baby. I'll touch base with you soon. Get yo' ass down there and keep me in tune. Later." He disconnected the call.

Fancii cried her heart out. She rocked back and forth on the floor until her nausea got the better of her. Then her head was in the toilet.

Mills rushed in and frowned. He was disgusted by the sight of her purging her guts. He thought about kicking her out of his parents' mansion. He no longer felt like dealing with her. She was becoming extra.

Fancii wiped her mouth with the back of her hand. "Mills, I need you to drive me to Sinai Samaritan hospital in Crenshaw. My brother has been shot. I have to get down there like right away," she said through a voice that was cracking up. She felt so weak and helpless. She stood and fell into his arms.

Mills caught her. He wrapped her into his arms, praying that he didn't catch whatever she was sick with. "Fancii, it's going to be okay. I got you. Let's get you down to the hospital right now."

Fancii broke into a fit of tears. "I don't want my brother to die, Mills. I can't take it if he does. He's all that I have left in this world. I don't even think I'm strong enough to see him in the condition that he's in." She hugged him tighter and sobbed loudly into his ear.

Mills grew more irritated. He knew that she was feeling weak, and in his mind, there was only one thing that would ease her pains and allow for her to get into a better state of mind. At the same time, it would cause her to fall under his control. With a woman as beautiful as Fancii under his thumb, he could do so many things. He could use her in any way that he needed to. But first, he had to conquer her as only he knew how. He hugged her tighter and kissed her forehead.

"Fancii, you're right. Look, there is no way that you're going to be able to go down there and do what you have to in the state of mind that you're in. But I got a li'l pick me upper that's going to help you feel all better. I'll be right back - I mean, if you want it?" he asked, hoping that she'd bite the bait.

Fancii felt so bad that she would have tried anything to make her sickness, and the pain in her heart, subside. "Just hurry, Mills. I'll try anything. I swear I will."

That was music to Mills's ears. It took all of his willpower not to form a huge smile across his face. A couple sniffs of the China and she would be his. He was humbly excited. "I'll be right back. You stay here."

Hood Rich

Chapter 2

It was five hours after Filipino's shooting. Noodles pulled his black-on-black 1987 Chevy Caprice Classic into Leimert Park and cut the headlights of his whip. He rolled down the long strip and made a left at the corner of Travis Street and took that block until he got to the middle of it.

Once there, he slowed the car. Up ahead he could see a group of dudes standing in front of an apartment building. Two parking spaces to the right of them was the van that had been used to gun down Filipino. He was sure now that it had, in fact, been Combo, and his crew that were responsible for his right-hand man's attack. He should have known.

He cocked the Mach Eleven and rolled down the window slowly. He slid the ski mask over his face and fixed it so that he could see properly through the eye holes. Then his foot eased off of the brake. The car wheeled into motion. "You know what? Fuck this drive-by shit. That's what bitches do." He threw the car in park and jumped out of it. Like a bat out of hell, he took off running in the direction of the group of niggas with the Mach in his hand. They were drinking forty ounce beers with brown paper bags over them, laughing and discussing the events that had taken place only hours ago with Combo.

"Man, that nigga was flopping around on that grass like a fish when them shells got to hitting his ass," one of them joked.

"Yeah, you wanna break a tough nigga down, you hit his ass with those hollows. This our city. Them fuck niggas gon' learn that shit one way or the other," another one said.

"We gotta catch Noodles though. That bitch nigga gotta feel these slugs. It's only right." He turned the St. Ides Premium up and got to guzzling.

Noodles sprinted down the sidewalk. He was thirsty for the kill. He could taste it. He had to avenge Filipino. Wasn't no nigga about to put slugs to his homie and get away with that.

One of the dudes lowered his bottle. He squinted at the distant figure running up on them. By the time he was able to focus, it was too late. He dropped the forty ounce and reached for his gun.

Noodles ran right up in them with his heart beating fast. "Bitch-ass niggas!"

Blocka-Blocka-Blocka.   *Blocka-Blocka-Blocka.*
Blocka-Blocka-Blocka.

His machine gun spit rapidly.

The bullets tore into the face of the dude that reached for his gun after he dropped his forty ounce. Noodles watched his brains blow out the back of his head. He was dead before he hit the ground. Noodles stepped on his dead body and kept on shooting. More bullets found their targets. Three more men from the group fell onto the pavement. Noodles stood over them and bucked them down. He watched their faces disappear as his bullets tore into them. A puddle of blood formed around their necks.

Most of the crew was able to run away, but that didn't stop Noodles from sending shots in their direction. He looked at the slain bodies on the ground and wished he could kill them all over again. He felt it was time that he turnt up. He and Filipino had given niggas one too many passes. It was over with for that shit. He jogged back to the car and stormed away from the scene with an unfulfilled feeling.

***

Fancii was high as a kite. Her entire body felt numb. She no longer felt sick. She felt like she was on top of the world, which was an odd feeling. She didn't know what Mills had encouraged her to snort, but whatever it was, it had done the trick. She stepped through the door and into the lobby of Sinai Samaritan. It seemed as if Sky spotted her right away. She rushed into her arms and hugged her tightly.

"Fancii, girl, oh my God. Your brother's in the Urgent Care unit. He was shot five times. But thankfully he had on a bulletproof vest. The main injuries that the doctors are worried about is the wound to his leg, and the one through his shoulder. They may have hit some vital arteries. They've already called for a blood transfusion," Sky uttered, hugging her.

Fancii suddenly felt weak again. "Why is this happening to our family? What have we done to deserve this? It seem like I was just here when my mother was killed. Now I'm back."

Sky put her arm around her neck and led her towards the waiting area. When she looked back, she saw the handsome Mills. "Uh, girl, who is that fine-ass light-skinned man right there?" she asked, nodding her head toward Mills.

Mills smiled. He waited for Sky to seat Fancii before he extended his hand. "How are you doing? My name is Mills Banks. I'm just a friend of Fancii's."

Sky shook his hand and couldn't take her eyes from his. He might have been the second finest black man she'd ever seen in her life. He ran neck in neck with Noodles. They even shared some of the same features. Both had tight, almond-shaped eyes, a muscular build, and a strong jawline and they were both tall, with a certain presence about themselves. "Wow, you're gorgeous. There is no way I could settle with being just your friend," Sky admitted. Even though she was shaken up from such a traumatic event, she couldn't deny the effects of his physical presence.

He laughed and stepped beside Fancii, knelt, and placed his arm around her shoulder. "You okay, Goddess?"

Sky watched him closely. She wondered what his and Fancii's true relationship really consisted of. Mills was too fine for any female to simply befriend. Fancii was known for being a goody-two-shoes. She, Cheyenne, and Fancii had all gone to Crenshaw High together, and before then, Kobe Bryant Middle school, so she was more than familiar with her customs and behaviors.

Before she could really figure their relationship out, Noodles came through the door with a mug on his face. He was dressed in all-black everything, all the way down to the black-on-black Jordans on his feet. He stormed across the lobby and stopped in mid-stride.

Sky looked him over curiously. Her head turned sideways of its own volition. "What the fuck is wrong with him?" she wondered.

Noodles stood there in the middle of the hospital waiting room, seething. Not only was there another man with his arm around his woman, but the man just so happened to be his brother by the father that had left him, his mother Sondra, and his sister Cheyenne behind so that he could seek greener pastures with the Italian woman he'd impregnated. The sight of Mills made him want to blow his brains out of his skull.

Fancii felt like she was being watched. Something told her to look up, and when she did, a cold chill ran down her spine. She jumped up, and the high from the China White seemed to discover her all over again. The sight of Noodles became fuzzy as he walked toward her in what appeared to be slow motion. "Noodles," she uttered

"Noodles?" Mills jumped up and became instantly defensive.

Noodles stepped into his face with his nostrils flared. "Fuck you doing with your arm around my woman, nigga? Don't yo' punk ass belong in Beverly Hills somewhere?"

Mills swallowed his spit. He dared to trail his eyes upward to Noodles's. "Big brother. How goes it, huh?"

Noodles pressed the tip of his nose against his. "Answer my fucking question, or you ain't about to make it back to Bel-Air, rich boy." Noodles meant every word that came out of his mouth. The way he was feeling he could have smoked Mills like a cigarette and thought nothing of it. The boy's very presence was a reminder of his father's betrayal to his first family. He hated the man and his seed that was Mills.

Fancii pushed them apart. "Hey, knock this shit off. I don't belong to no one other than myself. Noodles, you and I have a lot of stuff to work on, and we aren't doing it here. My brother is fighting for his fuckin' life right now. How about the two of you animals have some respect?" Fancii chastised, looking from one to the other. She couldn't believe that Mills Banks was Bronco Banks's son, as well as the brother of Noodles. She felt so stupid and wondered why she'd never made the connection before.

Noodles moved her out of the way. "Nigga, you fucked my bitch? Huh?"

Fancii felt offended. "Bitch? I know you ain't just call me a bitch, Noodles."

Mills was tired of playing pussy. He'd heard the stories about his older brother. He knew that he was an animal in the ghetto, somebody that nobody wanted to cross or screw around with. But he factored in that they were in a hospital and that there was nothing that Noodles could do to him in there unless he was out of his mind. Secondly, he couldn't allow himself to be punked in front of Fancii, or Sky. That was emasculating. "Say, I think you should watch yo' mouth when it comes to this Goddess right here. You wanna play that tough role, you can take that shit back into the streets of Crenshaw. We're dealing with a family crisis."

"Family? Nigga." Noodles swung as hard as he could and connected with Mills's jaw. He knocked him out with one punch.

Mills felt the monster punch. His head snapped backward, and everything went dark. His knees got weak, and he felt suddenly sleepy. The next thing he knew, he was dreaming.

Noodles stood over him. He hawked a loogey and spit it on him. "Fuck boy, this ain't no family of yours. Me and my homie grind these streets together every day, all day. He'll die for me, and I'll die for him. That's family." He kicked him in the ribs. "That's who you choosing over me? That's why you been acting all funny and shit? Yeah, a'ight then. I see what's really good. Sky, hit me up when you find something out about my mans." He rushed out of the hospital as he saw the security guard rounding the corner. He prayed the man didn't chase him. If he had to, he would blow his head off. Filipino's situation had him all screwed up mentally.

Sky's pussy instantly became wet. That thug shit did something to her that she couldn't explain. Noodles was her kryptonite. Her weakness. She wanted him so bad that she was willing to do anything to get him. She had to fan herself in order to calm down.

Fancii knelt beside Mills. She laid his head in her lap and rubbed his chest. "Mills. Mills. Wake up." She tapped his jaw. His bottom lip shook.

The white, older security guard rushed over to their side. "You guys alright over here? Should I go and call the real police?" he asked, looking terrified.

Sky giggled. "Yeah, we're good. Our friend just had a little fall. See, he's okay, he's waking up," Sky reported.

Mills opened his eyes. It felt like he had been hit with a sledgehammer. He didn't know where he was, or what was going on. The strong scent of women's perfume drifted up to his nose, arousing his inner man. He slowly sat up. "What happened?"

"You got yo' ass knocked out. That's what happened," Sky admitted.

"Sky? Damn, have a little class," Fancii snapped.

"You telling me. He should join a boxing class or something. I mean, bam, one punch and his ass was out like a light."

Mills grabbed his head in both of his big hands and shook it. He winced in pain. "That was a lucky fucking punch. It happens to the best of us." He made his way to his feet. He had to gather himself.

Fancii held him up. "You're okay, Mills. You don't have anything to prove. That was very immature of Noodles."

The security guard looked them over for a few more seconds. He wagged his finger at the trio. "No more problems tonight, you hear? This is a hospital, not a zoo."

"A zoo?" Sky smacked her lips. "Old man, you better keep it moving. Ain't no fucking animals up in here."

He waved her off. "Pipe down and get it together."

Fancii was offended as well, but she didn't feel like arguing or getting into trouble with the security guard. She was deathly worried about Filipino.

Sky took her earrings off, ready to give him a piece of her mind. "Excuse me, you racist son of a bitch!" she hollered.

A nurse stepped from the hallway into the waiting room. She looked around for Sky because Sky had been the one to say that she was Filipino's emergency contact. She spotted her. "Ma'am, I have some news concerning your brother. You may want to sit down for this."

Chapter 3
Two months later...

Filipino stood up from the dining room table and took a deep breath. He outstretched his right hand, balled it into a fist, and closed it again. Once again, it felt numb. Because of the gunshot to his right shoulder, the bullet had damaged nerves on his right side. Sometimes it made it hard for him to control it. He picked up the glass of water and held it for thirty seconds. Everything felt normal, and in the next second, he couldn't feel himself holding it anymore, but the glass remained in his grasp. He shook his head in mild irritation.

Noodles came up and rested his hand on one of his triceps. "It's all good, bruh. We gon' get you back right. We just gotta be thankful that you're alive. That's the most important thing to me. You feel me? Thank God for bulletproof vests." Noodles puffed on the big blunt and smiled at him.

Filipino nodded. He held the glass up toward the ceiling and looked it over closely. He sighed and lowered it. "Man, it done took me two months to get back to where I am now. I'm thankful for that. Them punk-ass people been sweating me though, Noodles. They been on my ass like a thong. We gotta get some chips just in case we get knocked and need a lawyer down the road. I ain't trying to be sitting in nobody's jail, fuck that." He took the blunt from Noodles, took three nice pulls, and inhaled the smoke deeply. He'd been smoking and popping pills more and more lately because of the incessant pain. His right thigh throbbed. It felt like his leg was about to go numb. He stomped his right foot, angry. "Man, Noodles. I'm sick of this shit though, cuz.

I gotta walk around fucked up for the rest of my life? Then we don't even know where that fuck nigga Combo chilling at. He could have took my life, homie. This shit far from over."

"Cuz, you already know that. Ain't nobody finna put no steel to you and think it's sweet. I been chopping down any nigga I think is close to him with no mercy. That fool can't run forever. Sooner or later, he gon' resurface. Los Angeles is all he knows, just like most of these hood niggas." Noodles took out two forty calibers and held them at his sides. "I ain't had nothing but money and murder on my mind ever since this shit happened to you, Filipino. I gotta get my head together though. We gotta get our chips right."

Filipino slightly limped into the kitchen and opened the refrigerator. He took out a quart of apple juice and brought it back into the dining room after grabbing two cups from the cupboard. "What's good wit' Sky? She ready for us to move or what?" He set the glasses on the dining room table and filled them halfway.

Noodles replaced his pistols. He grabbed one of the cups filled with juice and downed it. "We gon' meet with her old head tonight over dinner. Supposedly he got an offer for us. He says we can make some serious dough."

"How did you get involved with this stud again?" Filipino questioned with his right eyebrow raised.

"It wasn't me; it was all Sky. She told dude how when the shots were fired I dove on top of her and saved her life. She begged me to come and meet the old dude, and I'm glad that I did. On day one he put ten G's in my hand and gave me the keys to that 2019 Lexus out front. Told me I ain't owe him shit. That he owed me for saving his Brown Sugar. That when you got right, he wanted to meet you as well, and from there he would have some business arranged for us. Sky just sat back like a boss bitch and didn't utter a word. Her swag was terrific every time I hollered at this cat."

Filipino sat on the chair. "What's his name, Noodles?"

"It's gon blow yo' mind when I tell you who it is." Noodles felt some type of way.

"Who? Go ahead, spit that shit out," Filipino encouraged him anxious to know what what was.

"That Dwayne Haynes muthafucka."

"The mayor?" Filipino couldn't believe his ears.

Noodles nodded. "Yep. I know you done seen this dude a couple times in the hood."

"I thought Sky said her dude was white?"

Noodles shrugged his shoulders. "I guess she got more than one dude. Either way, this stud been looking out, and he wanna put some more on our plate. He could be talking about some serious chips. I say we have a sit down with him and see what's good. It's as simple as that."

Filipino frowned and felt confused. "Ain't the mayor like the head of law enforcement and all of that? Why would he be fucking around with Sky, or even us, for that matter? Ain't he supposed to be some kind of snob?"

Noodles shrugged his shoulders. "Didn't seem like it to me. He's a down-to-earth cat. He was raised in Crenshaw. You can take a nigga from Crenshaw out of the hood, but you can't take the hood out of a nigga from Crenshaw."

Filipino laughed. "We gon' be the same way when we make it big, Noodles. We gon' have major money but still be down-to-earth and hood as hell. You getting what I'm saying?"

Noodles nodded. He couldn't wait until they finally made it out of the trenches of South Los Angeles. He wanted a better life for his mother and sister. He was tired of his mother having to endure the random drive=by shootings, gang violence, rats, and roaches. He wanted to move her to a nice spot in Beverly Hills, or even the Valley. A place where she would never have to worry about losing her life just because she wanted to go to the grocery store. He wanted better for Cheyenne as well. Whenever he moved his mother, he would see to it that Cheyenne came along for the ride. In his opinion, there was nothing left in Crenshaw for her either. Ever since they had been a part of the community, there had been nothing but pain and agony. He was tired of it. Dwayne seemed as if he had a road that led out of Crenshaw, and Noodles was looking to take it. "Filipino, get fitted. We finna go holler at this dude in a couple hours. He sending a limo to pick us up."

"Shid, say no mo'," Filipino quipped, excited.

***

Three hours later, Noodles leaned back into the soft, white leather seats of the stretch Cadillac Escalade. He held a bottle of Rosé that had been chilled just right, and in his left hand was a fat blunt of Maui Loud. He was fitted in Burberry from head to ankle, over a pair of custom-designed retro seven Jordans. They also had the Burberry logo on them.

Filipino popped three Perc thirties, chewed them, and washed them down with his bottle of Ace of Spades. The powder was strong in his mouth. It tasted horrible. He squeezed his eyelids together. He prayed the effects of the drug kicked in right away. His right shoulder was killing him. Every time he moved it in the slightest, a stinging pain resonated all the way down to his wrist and back up. His fingers felt numb on his right hand. That didn't stop him from dressing to the nines. He was fitted in Gucci, all the way down to his custom-designed Gucci Air Force Ones. They were the first Jordans that had ever come out, retro status. They had Gucci's logo all over them.

"How you holding up?" Noodles asked. He felt breezy. The stretch limousine turned around a bend and made its way through a beach in Malibu. The sun was just beginning to set. Noodles eyed the white women that were taking part in a game of volleyball. They wore thongs all up their asses. Their breasts bounced up and down on their slim figures. The ocean's water looked bright and blue. He found it funny that even the ocean looked better and healthier on the rich people side of Los Angeles.

Filipino rotated his shoulder. A sharp pain shot up and nearly caused him to holler out in pain. He took a deep breath. "Bruh, I'm fucked up. It ain't enough pills in the world to take this pain away from me. That nigga Combo fucked me up. I'm probably gon' have to deal with this for the rest of my life." He shook his head. He could feel the bulletproof vest cling tight to his body. Ever since the attack, he'd worn one as if it were a second skin. It was because of the vest that he still had life in his body.

Noodles got heated. "That chump ain't gon' get away with this shit. Every dog has its day. Sooner or later that punk gon' meet this wrath. When he do, we gon' shoot so that a vest can't even save his ass." Noodles imagined what gunning Combo down would feel like. A sinister smile spread across his face.

Filipino took a long swallow from his champagne and wiped his mouth with the back of his hand. "Fuck shooting, Cuz. I wanna enjoy killing that nigga. I wanna cut his ass up in little bitty pieces, then make him eat hisself before he die. I ain't never hate nobody as much as I hate this clown. This nigga fucked me up, Cuz."

Noodles nodded his head as the limo stopped at a big, black metal gate. The driver punched in a series of numbers, then placed his hand on the digital screen. It beeped five times. Then the gate clicked and slid sideways loudly.

"That's some boss shit right there," Filipino uttered, amused. He watched the gate close behind them. He sat back in his seat as the limo rounded the path and headed toward the three-story mansion.

Noodles's eyes bucked, yet he was determined. He felt deep in his heart that one day he was going to have a mansion as massive as the one that they were set to walk inside. The ghetto was only a temporary chain that was wrapped around his ankle. His ultimate goal was to break away from it. Nothing and no one would stop him from doing so.

The limo came to a halt right in front of the mansion's door. The driver threw the truck in park and made his way around to the back doors. He opened the one that Noodles sat closest to and stepped out of the way.

Noodles's Jordans stepped on the pavement, then he was standing tall. A light breeze brushed across his face. He looked the red brick mansion over and grew a bit envious. He felt like the home should have been where his mother Sondra and sister Cheyenne rested their heads. They deserved a safe haven like the one he was looking at. His mother deserved to feel safe and sound every night. She shouldn't have to worry about the deadly unknown. As a man, he would get her a mansion. As a man, he felt that was his place.

Filipino stepped out and looked the mansion over. "So that's what the mayor staying in? Shid, I gotta get into politics." He laughed. Filipino knew that he would never reach such a success. His vision for success was being able to make it through the day without being murdered. Now that all he had left was his sister, he didn't know how to function goal-wise. He didn't know what he wanted out of life. His mother was his focal point. With her being gone, he yearned for direction. So, in the meantime, it was all about stacking as much money as feasibly possible.

The doors to the mansion opened and two big buff security guards stepped out of the doors. They posted up on each side and crossed their arms. From the middle of the men stepped Dwayne. He was dressed in a navy blue Italian suit with the matching Gucci loafers. He was dark-skinned, tall, with graying waves on his head. His cologne was strong. He extended his hand and walked toward Noodles. They shook. "Li'l brother. It's good to see you again. I hope the ride was comfortable for you."

Noodles shook his hand and nodded his head. "Yeah, I can get used to rolling in something like that. I felt like a boss the whole time."

"And this is how you should be rolling, li'l brother. You shouldn't have to worry about nothing, especially when it comes to being comfortable. That's why we need to have this sit down. It's imperative that we do so."

Filipino sized him up. "This here is a duo, Mr. Haynes. You talking to by brother like I ain't apart of this equation or something." Filipino felt offended. In his eyes, he and Noodles were blood. He didn't care how much money and power the mayor had. He wasn't about to break that up.

Dwayne smiled and extended his hand to Filipino. "Oh no, suh. You see, the reason why this meeting didn't take place any sooner is because I wanted to wait until you recovered as much as you could." He looked him up and down. "You look good to me. Oh, and those legal troubles? Forget about them. Fellas, follow me."

Filipino watched Noodles walk behind the man. He stood dumbfounded as the sun set directly to the west of him. What legal troubles was the man talking about? He jogged and caught up with them.

When they stepped into the mansion, the first thing Noodles saw was a fountain directly in the center of the huge living room. There were two flights of stairs that led to the upstairs portion of the house. To their left was an elevator. Directly down the center of the mansion was the big kitchen, and to the left of that was a long hallway. There were paintings all over the mansion of famous Black Americans. Two dark-skinned female maids waited just outside of the kitchen. They were dressed in Gucci maid uniforms. They didn't look older than twenty-five. Noodles had to admit to himself that both of the sistas were gorgeous.

Dwayne held out his arm. "You fellas should follow me right this way." He walked ahead of them. When they got in front of the maids, he stopped. "Are either one of you li'l brothers hungry? These Queens cook some of the best soul food this side of California."

Filipino stepped forward and took the hand of one of the sistas. He kissed the back of it. "Mama, you are gorgeous. I can't see you cooking for no other nigga but me."

She laughed and took her hand away. "Boy, you silly."

"Nall, I'm serious," he assured her.

Dwayne placed his hand on his shoulder. "Trust me, li'l brother, you can't afford her yet. Baby girl, tell him what I just bought you for your birthday."

She smiled. "A Rolls Royce, and three carat earrings priced at fifty thousand dollars. To be honest, those are the weakest gifts I've ever gotten from him. He can be quite generous when he wants to be." She eyed Dwayne seductively.

Filipino was dumbfounded. He stood there with his mouth wide open. "Yeah, I can't fuck wit' you in that tip. They say it ain't tricking if you got it. Well, I ain't tricking 'cause I ain't got it." He stepped past her. "Let's get on with this meeting. That shit just irritated me."

Noodles laughed and shook his head. "Sound like a plan bruh." He pat his back.

Dwayne stepped up to the female whose hand Filipino had kissed. He whispered in her ear so that neither Filipino nor Noodles could hear him. "Say baby, you see these two li'l niggas right there? They gon' help me to stay in my mayoral seat, so I want you to be nice to both of them Kandi, you, and your sister. Put that pussy on him, play wit' his mind. Game that nigga. Earn that ma'fuckin' Phantom. Now." He casually stepped away from her.

Kandi cleared her throat. She reached and took ahold of Filipino's wrist. "Say baby, ain't no reason for you to get upset. Before you leave, you and I are going to get well acquainted. How does that sound?"

Filipino raised his right eyebrow and looked back at Dwayne. "Damn, it's like that?"

Dwayne smiled. "It's just like that."

Chapter 4

Dwayne paced back and forth inside of the boardroom. "So, what I'm saying is this. Somebody has waged a war against me. They are looking to take me out of my seat as mayor here in Los Angeles. They are purposely raising the crime rate, attacking and destroying the places that I was looking to turn into neighborhood centers. They are robbing the businesses on Jefferson Boulevard. Crenshaw Plaza has also seen an increase in crime. So has the Leimert district. Drug houses have sprung up out of nowhere. And I'm not talking soft drugs like crack or marijuana. I'm talking the harsh shit. The stuff that gets the people uttering the need for a new leader loudly. Uttering that I can't use right now. But it's all by design. None of this is a coincidence. The practice to inflate the crime rate during an election year has been used since the beginning of time. I don't knock it. It's a part of the game."

He wiped his mouth and folded the sleeves back on his suit shirt. "But anyway, now I could use the police. Everybody knows that LAPD is a son of a bitch. I could have them pulling kick doors and getting overly aggressive with the locals until we squeeze these punks out. But then I run the risk of more lawsuits and public scrutiny. It's a tough game, this political field, but it's a game that I intend to win." He ran his hand over his waves.

Filipino blew a cloud of weed smoke to the ceiling. He kicked his Jordans up on the table. "So how the fuck we finna help you?"

Noodles sat listening in attentively. He wanted to hear and analyze every word that came out of Dwayne's mouth. He felt that the smartest way to master any situation, or anything, was to know it inside and out. He needed to know Dwayne's motives. He saw that he was speaking from an emotional standpoint. The best way to figure out a man's motives were when he was in his most emotional state of mind. Anger was the enemy of its beholder. Noodles knew this.

Dwayne mugged Filipino and caught himself. He could tell that Filipino was all street, with very little brains. No doubt, he would be used as an assassin. Or the front man. Dwayne was sure that when he was done with the use of both men that he was going to make sure they were murdered and never heard from again. He already disliked Filipino. He felt the thug was way too cocky considering he was so young and broke. He scoffed and turned his back to them. "I am going to use you two to push back against my destroyers. I have C.I.'s that have given me enough intel to let me know that a war has been waged against me by this peasant right here." He flipped on the projector, and a picture of Bronco Banks graced the screen. He wore a three piece business suit and carried a crocodile briefcase. "You boys know who this is?"

Noodles stiffened in his seat. He looked over his father on the screen. An utter disdain came upon him. In five seconds, he was angry. The sight of the man caused his blood to feel as if it were boiling. Still he remained silent.

Filipino looked over at Noodles. Since he didn't answer the question, he didn't either. "What about him?"

Dwayne tapped the projection screen. "This is my destroyer. This is the man that is directly behind me in the polls. According to my informants, he is also the one that has waged a war against me in order to oust me from my seat. He is my enemy, and what better way to go at your enemy than to use his son against him?" He smiled and looked into Noodles's eyes.

Noodles felt the hairs stand up on his arms. So, the mayor knew. He knew that Bronco Banks was his father, and he intended to use Noodles to clap back at him. Noodles didn't know how he wanted him to do it, but he was all for it. As long as it was going to be beneficial for his family.

Filipino stood up. He was shocked and angered. "That's what all of this shit is about, you getting revenge on Bronco by using the homie? Nigga, you nuts. Bruh ain't in no shit like that."

"Noodles, what do you want more than anything else in life?"

Noodles adjusted himself in the comfortable leather chair. "To move my mother and sister out of the hood."

"How does a four bedroom house in the Valley sound?" He pulled out his phone. "This place has a big front yard, a swimming pool in the back. Comes with a 2020 Lexus sedan. No rent, no mortgage, you sign on with me, it's yours. We can move your mother out of Crenshaw and to the Valley in less than four months. All I ask is that you join this fight with me. Let me also sweeten the pot a bit more. Listen, there are a series of destroyers that Bronco has hired. I want you guys to take care of each one of them. You'll be raiding their spots and keeping the loot. All of it. I won't micromanage what you do during the process. All I ask is that no bodies be dropped or found in South Los Angeles. I need for you to get the message through to these bandits that working for Bronco Banks is the wrong move. Crime has to drop, and it has to drop drastically in order for me to maintain my seat. In addition, I'll be issuing the both of you ten thousand a week for your assistance. Do we have a deal?"

"Hell n'all, that's still my nigga's father. He ain't gon' - " Filipino started.

"Let's do it," Noodles interrupted.

Filipino was shocked. "You sure, bruh?"

Noodles stood up. "Fuck Bronco. That fool ain't doing nothing for my family, so it's up to me to. Mr. Haynes has given us an opportunity to get right. I mean, we was gon' be pulling kick downs anyway, might as well get a li'l backing from him. I'm all in. What is step one?"

Dwayne stepped over to his laptop and pulled up a list of contacts from Crenshaw and other impoverished surrounding areas that Bronco Banks's camp had made contact with over the last few months. He printed them out and gave a sheet to both Filipino and Noodles. "These are some if the addresses. I've already marked what each spot is set to be holding, and what they are selling out of the residences. Use it to make your jobs easier. We'll report back here once a week each Friday for updates. You guys get those numbers down, and I'll make you young kings. That's my word." He tapped a button on his desk.

Noodles shook his hand. "I got this shit. Me and the homie gon' handle this bidness. Believe that."

"I know you will, Nadell. I have the utmost faith in you."

The door to the boardroom opened. In stepped Kandi and her sister Brandi. Instead of being dressed in the maid uniforms, they were adorned in white stockings with garters attached to them. Up above were Prada corsets. They rocked all-black Christian Dior pumps.

Filipino grew alert right away. "Now this what the fuck I'm talking about." He stepped to Kandi and slid his arms around her waist. He took ahold of her ass and squeezed the cheeks. "Damn, you strapped, shawty."

She moaned and sucked his neck. "We can do whatever you wanna do, daddy. I been feeling your swag from the moment I laid eyes on you." She licked along the length of the thick vein that decorated his neck.

Filipino didn't waste any time at all. His fingers traveled underneath the thong strip that covered her asshole. He traveled down to her pussy and played over the plump lips. She was shaved bald. He could even feel the slight crinkles along her folds.

Brandi stepped into Noodles's glamour. They were face to face. Her chocolate skin popped in the light. "I'm saying, daddy. I know we ain't about to let them do their thing without us handling out bidness. That don't even make any sense to me. Especially because you're fine as ever." She gripped his dick through his pants. It felt like a thick cucumber. She squeezed and it throbbed.

Noodles moaned. It had been over two months since he'd gotten some pussy. The situation with Fancii was fresh in his brain. He missed her. He still thought about her, and on top of that, he still loved her. He pushed Brandi slightly out of his way. "Hold fast, shawty, I'm fucking wit' somebody already."

Filipino picked Kandi up and set her on the table. He had two fingers buried deep within her cleft. "My sister fuckin' wit' that rich nigga now, Noodles. She ain't thinking about you no more, Cuz. Both of these bitches fine. I say you smash shawty, and then we switch." He lifted Kandi's left thigh on his shoulder and continued to rub her pussy. It got wet, began to leak. He could smell her perfumed, yet earthly scent. He wanted into that pussy. His fingers ran in and out of her at full speed.

Brandi dropped to her knees. She rubbed her hand over his pants front. "Don't worry, baby. I ain't trying to marry you. I'm just trying to set your mind at ease." She peeled his jean buttons apart and pulled out his big dick. It looked like a swollen brown pickle. The head was dark purple. Small veins went through it. It was the biggest piece that she had ever seen in her twenty-three years of living. She stroked it up and down. Her pussy quivered. A trace of juice seeped out of her box and slid down her thigh.

The more she worked his dick, the hornier Noodles became. He wanted to fuck something so bad. No, not something. He wanted to fuck Fancii so bad. He took a step back and pulled up his pants. "I can't fuck wit' you like that, shawty. Like I said, I'm fuckin' wit' somebody already."

Filipino slid into Kandi's hot pussy after rolling the Magnum over his pipe. Her lips opened and sucked him in. Her tunnel was tight. Welcoming. He slammed his dick all the way home, pulled out, only to slam home again and again. The pussy felt like it got better and better. He pushed her knees to her chest and started to wreck her.

"Un. Un. Un. Fuck. Fuck. Oooh. Slow down. Slow down. Awwww. Yes. Yes. Oooh shit. Oooh shit. He fuckin' me. He fuckin' me." She threw her head back and took Filipino's pounding. His dick was wide, the head huge. She could feel her hole opening up for his assaults.

Filipino dragged her backward on the table. He climbed upon it and really got to tearing her ass up. His dick was like a battering ram. Her pussy juice ran out of her and into the crack of her ass, where his balls slapped into the liquids. "Fuck, bitch. Fuck. I knew it. Argh. I knew. She. Had. Some. Bomb. Ass. Pussy!" Harder and harder he fucked with no mercy.

Kandi's tongue traced her lips. Her eyes had been closed, but she opened them and saw how Brandi looked so intently at her being fucked by Filipino. She looked jealous. Her nipples poked through the material of her top. Though Dwayne was a cash cow, he was nothing more than a bore in the bedroom. Neither woman could remember the last time they'd been fucked in the manner that Filipino was fucking Kandi. Kandi felt Filipino slam into her deeply, and she screamed. She came all over his dick, shaking as if she was having a seizure. The sexing felt so incredibly good to her. "Uhhhhhhhh! Shiiit!"

Filipino watched his pole run in and out of her. He continued to bang. He felt the semen rising in his balls. He pulled off his condom and came all over her chocolate stomach in big white globs.

Brandi's knees buckled. She whimpered and fell to the floor. Her pussy was jumping and leaking at the same time. As soon her fingers touched her clit, she came, shivering against the side of the table. She whimpered and could not take her eyes off the sight of Filipino's member. She envied Kandi, and detested Noodles for denying her the same pleasures her sister had experienced.

Dwayne placed his hand on Noodles's shoulder. "Listen to me, son, I know this entire ordeal hits close to home for you. Just know that I have you. My goal is to make sure that I remain in my seat, and that as a result, you and your family are well taken care. It's as simple as that. Sorta, one hand washes the other. Understand? Any utensils you'll need to complete these tasks, I'll make sure that you have them. There's simply one last thing." He paused to watch Brandi take ahold of Filipino's piece. She kissed his head and slipped it into her mouth. In no time, she was spearing her face into his lap. Dwayne smiled. He loved both sisters. They were pure sluts. Uninhibited. Just the way he liked them. "Anyway, under no circumstances can whatever you're doing in the field get back to me. I will do my part to ensure that you're always given a heathy amount of lead way, but if I should stumble, you guys have to hold your weight until I can figure some things out from behind the scenes. Do you get that?" He asked this question looking into Noodles's eyes.

Noodles glared at him, then lowered his own eyes into slits. He didn't like what the man was getting at. He brushed his hand off of his shoulder. "Say, Dwayne, if you're insinuating what I think you are, you can miss me with that bullshit. Me and my nigga know how to hold our own weight. If we get bumped in the field, we'll handle that shit when it happens. None of this will ever report back to you. We from the trenches, old head, don't get that shit twisted."

Dwayne took a step back and held up in hands at shoulder length. "Whoa, I didn't mean no disrespect. I just wanted to let you know what I was thinking, that's all."

"Right, and I just did the same thing." He turned to see Filipino bend Brandi over, then he was sliding into her and piping her down at full speed while he and Kandi made out loudly. "Bruh, after you down that bitch, we up out of here. We got our understanding." He glanced at Dwayne from the corners of his eyes.

Hood Rich

Chapter 5

Mills slowly made his way down the hallway with the tray of breakfast. He was dressed in a pair of Gucci pajamas, and still had his wave cap on his head. He came to the guestroom door and knocked on it. Tomorrow was his eighteenth birthday, and he would officially become the owner of Club Flawless. But today would be the first day he showed Fancii around the club. She'd already agreed to become his hostess. He was excited about having her around amongst the other girls.

Fancii stretched her arms over her head and yawned. The silk sheets fell off of her body. She opened her eyes and looked around the room. She still couldn't believe that she'd been blessed to sleep inside of the massive palace once again. "Who is it?"

Mills turned the knob and stepped into the room. On the tray alongside of the food was a small vase with a single red rose inside of it. "Good morning, baby. Open them pretty li'l eyes and bless the world with your beauty." He brought the tray to the night table beside her and placed it there. He looked down on her and knelt on the bed.

Fancii felt insecure. She could taste that her breath was a little tart. She ran her hand over her face to ensure that there was no cold in her eyes. "Mills, thank you. Wow, you didn't have to do all of that." She glanced over the tray of food hungrily. She saw Eggs Benedict, French toast, three sausages, a small bowl of oatmeal, and a tall glass of orange juice. It all looked so good. Fancii's body began to ache out of the blue. "Uh, Mills." She hugged herself. "Did you happen to bring me some..."

45

Mills smiled. Now this was the greeting that he was looking for. "I may have, but what you got for me?" he teased.

Fancii ran her fingers through her hair and shook. "What do you want?" She batted her eyelashes and sucked on her bottom lip.

Mills took the small Ziploc bag of China White out of his pajama pocket. He shook it in front of her and sat back and watched the effects the sight of the drug had on her. It always amused him.

Fancii felt weak. Her stomach did a somersault. Her body felt like it was aching. She came to her knees and bucked her eyes. She yearned for a taste of the drug. Her nose began to run. She sniffed as hard as she could to return the snot. "Mills, what do you want. Huh?" Her hand eased into his lap. She rubbed. Clutched his penis with her right hand. "Please tell me."

Mills felt his dick rise. He leaned back in the bed and watched her fish out his log. She stroked it, squeezed it in her small fist, and pulled down on it. Her tongue ran across her lips. She opened her mouth and sucked him into it. The entire time her pretty brown eyes focused in on his own. "Damn, baby," he moaned. "Shit." He rested his hand on the back of her head.

Fancii sucked and tugged. His penis was hard in her mouth. She took it as far inside as she could, pulled back, and then sucked down it again. She wanted the drug. Needed it. Her emotions were a ball of chaos. She was starting to ache from missing her mother again. Aching from the devastation of the world. The pressure of it all. But the heroin would ease her discomforts. It would place her into a better state of mind, if only for a moment. All she had to do was to make him cum first.

After he came, he would be at her disposal. The thought made her add more spit and suck harder. She moaned around it.

Mills's toes curled. He groaned and squeezed his eyelids together. He fucked into her mouth faster and faster, humping upward from the bed. Fancii's head game was phenomenal the way her tongue made circles around his crown before taking the length of him, the way she added just the right amount of spit, the way she peered into his eyes, almost daring him to cum inside of her mouth. Yeah, for Mills, she was the shit. He felt her nip at him with her teeth lightly, and he started to cum. "Shit. Shit. I'm cumming. I'm cumming. Fuck," he moaned, busting back to back.

Fancii pulled his dick out and jerked it. She allowed the nut that shot into the air. It came back down and landed around her fist. She licked it up and continued to pump him before sucking him back into her mouth.

Mills's eyes rolled into the back of his head. He was breathing hard. His dick went from being semi-erect to rock hard. Fancii had that effect on him. He reached over her back and squeezed her ass. "You gon' give me some of this pussy this morning, huh?" He fingers trailed down her ass crack. They wound up in her crease, right over her pussy lips that were molded to her pajama pants.

Fancii spread her knees. "Mills. Is that what you want, baby? Huh? You want some of this Asian and Black pussy?" She licked up and down his shaft.

Mills pushed the material into her pussy lips. They instantly became wet. He rubbed them furiously. Squeezed them together. "Yeah, baby. Hose me with that body." He scooted up some more and pulled his Gucci pajamas all the way off.

Fancii stood at the foot of the bed. She pulled the Prada pajama pants down her thighs. Stepped out of them. Her pussy juice ran down her thighs. She crawled across the bed and straddled his lap. There was nothing but the drug on her mind. It dominated her every thought with the exception of the strategy it took to obtain the delights of the China White. She tried to kiss his lips, but Mills turned his head. He didn't want to taste his own semen that he was sure was on her tongue. All he wanted was the pussy. Her box was nice and tight, and always wet. Fancii opened her lips and felt his dick head sliding between them. She slowly slid backwards until she engulfed him entirely. When she was sitting on his nuts, she moaned. "Okay, baby, let's get it."

Mills gripped her fat ass and allowed her to ride him. Her pretty breasts bounced up and down inside of her shirt. He gripped them, and then with a tug, ripped it wide open, spilling the buttons all over the bedroom. Her titties spilled out. He forced her downward while he sucked in each huge areola.

Fancii rolled her back. She rode him faster and faster with the drug on her mind. She needed him to cum. The faster he came, the quicker she would be able to obtain the China White that he held over her head. She needed it. Yearned for it. "Uh! Mills! Oooh," she growled. Faster and faster her pussy sucked at him.

Mills held her ass and couldn't believe how good the kitty felt. It poured all over his lap. She bounced higher and came down harder. Her nails dug into his chest. The scent of their fucking wafted into the air.

Fancii took a hold of the headboard and popped her ass. His dick traveled deeper and deeper into her box. It even hurt just a little bit. It reminded her of all of the times she had been with Noodles, her first and only love. The image of him came into her mind. She tried to hold it. The more she was able to, the easier it was for her to screw Mills. She rode him faster, imagining that it was Noodles. "Uhhh! Uhhh! Baby! Baby!"

Mills gripped that ass harder. He felt her walls sucking at him. Milking him. His eyes crossed. He opened his mouth wide and groaned. Then he was cumming splash after splash into her tight, swampy, sex.

Fancii felt the semen gunning for her walls. That brought on her own climax. "Shit! Shit! Noodles. Noodles. Aw, fuck me!" she screamed, cumming on top of Mills. As soon as she finished the words, she felt a cold chill run down her spine. She continued to cum, shaking like crazy.

Mills finished his last spurts and pushed her off of him. He jumped up with cum and her juices all over his hard piece. "Noodles? That's who you were thinking about while we were together?" he snapped.

Fancii saw a trail of juice leak from his rock hard shaft. She shook her head. "No, baby. I was cumming. My brain was haywire. Before you, Noodles was the only other man I've ever been with. So, it was like my brain was on autopilot. He's never made me cum like that though," she lied. Noodles had been the only person to ever give her back-to-back orgasms on a regular basis. She missed him.

Mills frowned. He pointed at her. "Fancii, I swear to God, you better get your shit in order, or you're going to be back in the ghetto with all of that shooting and poverty shit. You got a good thing here. You need to wake up and see that." He turned his back to her, picked his pants up off of the floor, and slipped them on. "Get dressed. We'll be leaving in an hour." He got ready to leave the room.

She hopped out of the bed and caught him and grabbed his wrist. "Baby, wait, you gotta get me right. You gotta take care of me. Give me a little taste. Come on now, I need it. My body is starting to ache. I'm feeling sick."

Mills yanked his wrist away. "Oh yeah? Then why don't you go and ask Noodles for a taste. I'm sure he'll fulfill that need, since he fulfills all the other ones." Mills rolled his eyes like a broad and made his way out of the room.

Fancii jumped on his back. She wrapped her legs around his waist. "Please, please, please, Mills. I swear it wasn't what you thought. You're overreacting. All I see is you. You're my every thought. You drive me crazy. Now get me right, baby. Please. I am begging you."

Mills carried her over to the bed and flung her off of him. He mugged her for a long time. He wanted to be disgusted by her, but the sight of her drove him crazy. Her long hair was all over her face. She had her thighs slightly parted so he could see her thick pussy lips as they glistened. Her scent was heavenly to him. He wanted to kick her ass out of Bel-Air, but he couldn't. She had ahold on him.

Besides, the fact that she craved Noodles only made him want her more. She was a project. For once in his life, she was something that he would have to work hard for. He pulled the dope back out of his pajama pocket.

"Awright then, I got you." He closed the door to the bedroom all the way and knelt in front of the night stand. He moved the platter of breakfast out of the way and dumped out about a gram of the China White. He separated it into four thin lines and took a step back. He pointed at it.

Fancii nearly broke her neck to get over there. "Thank you, baby. Thank you so much." She threw her hair over her shoulders. She looked back at him once again and got ready to snort.

Mills grabbed a handful of her hair and yanked her head back so hard that a bone in her neck popped. "Tell me you belong to me! Say it! Say it now, bitch!"

Fancii craved the drug. She would say anything. "I belong to you. I belong to you."

Mills slapped her across the face and knocked her to the floor. "Bitch, don't you ever hurt my feelings like that again, do you hear me? You ever hurt me like that again, we gon' have a major problem. You understand that?" He grabbed her by the pajama top and put his forehead against hers. "Do you?"

Fancii swallowed her spit. She could feel a slight trickle of blood slide down the side of her lip. "Yes, baby, I understand you. I understand you. I swear I do." Her body craved the poison.

Mills released her and stood back. "Get yo' ass over there and treat your nose. You earned that. You almost lost it, but you earned it for now. If I ever catch my brother's name on your tongue again while we're doing our thing, the next time I won't be so nice." His heart beat hard in his chest. He was riled up. He pointed. "Go."

Fancii trembled and crawled across the floor. She made it to the night table and sighed with relief. She opened the drawer that was attached to the table and took out a golden straw. In a matter of seconds, she vacuumed the drug into her nose. She pinched her nostrils and tilted her head back. The numb feeling engulfed her at once. Then the music started to play inside of her head. A soft melody. A soothing, comforting melody that slowly allowed for her body to float off of the ground. Her head began to spin. She was consumed by a strong euphoric covering. The sickness that had overtaken her before immediately subsided. A broad smile spread across her face. She cleared another line that pushed her high over the top. Suddenly she felt as if nothing else in the world mattered. Nothing mattered more than the lines of China White that took her on a journey through the gates of heaven.

Mills looked on, amused. He nodded his head. "Yeah, I got this bitch. She's mine. I'll show Noodles. I'ma show him who runs this shit."

He walked over and sat on the bed and pulled her thighs apart. He slid his hand between her legs and rubbed her pussy. "Hurry up, baby. I want some more of this box."

Chapter 6

A week later, at eleven o'clock Friday afternoon, Noodles pulled into the parking lot of Leimert Park and cut his headlights. He made sure that he parked a safe distance away from the basketball courts. Currently there was a game taking place. Five on five. That made ten people taking part in the game, and there were three females on the sidelines cheering them on.

Filipino cocked the automatic shotgun. He glanced over to the courts. "So, you telling me that however many of these ma'fuckas we hit, we gotta pick their bodies up and then transport their asses to any side of town other than the south side of Los Angeles?"

Noodles pulled a Mach Ninety from under his seat and slammed a hundred round magazine inside of it. He cocked it from the top and nodded. "Yep, that's what it is. That's why I'm rolling this van. We can't add to the body count on this side of town. These are where his votes are going to come from, so he wants us to make the west side and east side crime rates rise. Those will be our dump sights. We needed targets. All of them bitch niggas over there fuck wit' Combo. They work for him. Just because we working for Dwayne, that don't mean that we ain't on a mission to fuck over these niggas that put you down. Never that. The money is cool, but my first loyalty is to you, bruh, you already know that shit."

"What's understood need not be expressed. The feeling is most definitely mutual. But what about them bitches though? We fucking them over too?" Filipino didn't mind slugging anybody. If they fucked wit' Combo, he wanted to take a good look at them.

"You should avoid hitting them as best as you can, but if one of them hoes gets to bucking, you already know bullets ain't got no names on them." He pulled a Wolverine mask over his face and slid on his black leather gloves.

Filipino put on a Black Panther mask. "That sounds good to me. I'm finna put a bunch of these Wakandas in they ass," he joked, trying to tie together the Black Panther movie and their current war situation. "You ready?"

Noodles nodded. He threw the van in drive and slowly pulled up alongside of the gate where the game was taking place. There was only one exit out of the basketball courts, and the fence was at least twenty feet high. They would for sure be able to finish the job before any one of the culprits were able to. He drove up on the curb and hopped it. He slammed on the brakes just as the body of the van blocked the exit of the basketball courts.

Filipino slid the side door back and rushed onto the courts. Somebody yelled, "It's a hit." It was like everything began to go in slow motion. The players on the court started to disburse in every direction. Filipino brought the shotgun shoulder level, closed his left eye, and aimed.

Bocka. Bocka. Bocka.

His first three bullets hit their intended targets. Three dudes caught back shots. They fell to the ground face first and laid straight out. The bullets had taken their lives on impact.

Noodles finger fucked his trigger.

Blocka. Blocka. Blocka. Blocka.

He ran spitting. His bullets chopped down five dudes in less than ten seconds. They lay on the pavement twisted, shaking with blood pouring out of them. He felt no mercy. It was killa season in his mind. Combo had opened up a can of worms, and now his people were suffering the consequences until he felt it was time to emerge and end the war that he'd waged against Filipino and Noodles.

Filipino rushed up to the gate as one dude made his way halfway up it. He aimed with his shotgun and fired. The bullet traveled at lightning speed. It slammed into the enemy's back and knocked him from the gate. He fell to the gravel, lifeless. Filipino stood over him and smiled.

The last three were huddled into a corner of the gate. Noodles walked up to them with his gun aimed. "Move and you die. Where the fuck is Combo? Where that nigga hiding at?" He demanded an answer.

A light-skinned female with freckles all over her face spoke up. "He's recovering in Oakland. After he got popped fucking with some niggas from Crenshaw, the next night some niggas rolled down on him while he was getting wheeled out of the hospital and hit him up twice. He fucking around at his brother's crib out in Oakland."

"Bitch, shut up!" the last dude present hollered.

Filipino walked up to him and pulled the trigger. The bullet lifted him off of his feet and threw him into the gate. He fell down it and slid to his ass, slumped over with his head between his legs. "Bitch nigga."

The girls screamed and hugged each other. Both were shaking horribly. They didn't want to die, not because of enemies of Combo.

"Please," the light-skinned chick spoke again. "I got the address and everything. I'll help you catch him. Just don't hurt me or my li'l cousin right here."

Noodles, looked over to Filipino. "What you think, homie?"

Filipino scratched the side of his head with the barrel of his shotgun. "I don't know, Cuz. Wait, do both of you hoes know where he at?"

The dark-skinned girl shook her head. "I'm from Las Vegas. I don't know what's going on with none of this. My cousin told me to come out here so we could fuck wit' some niggas, and - "

Filipino raised his shotgun and fired, knocking her head from her shoulders. She did a one eighty in the air and fell on her back. "Bitch can't help us none."

The light-skinned chick screamed. "Ahh. Ahh. Oh my God. Oh my God. Oh my God, please don't kill me," she begged.

Noodles grabbed her by the throat. "You not only gon' give me his address, but you gon' show me where this nigga at. If not, yo' head gon' be lying next to hers. You see that, bitch?" He tilted her so she could look down at her cousin.

"Okay. Okay. Okay. I will. Just please don't hurt me. I am begging you."

Filipino swung and connected with her chin. As soon as his knuckles connected and he followed through, she was out like a light.

Before she could hit the ground, Noodles caught her and picked her up. He tossed her on to his shoulder. "Bruh, drag them bodies over to the van. We gotta hurry up before Twelve get in route. When this bitch wake up, she finna take us to this nigga. That's how that's finna go."

***

Mills sat back on the red leather couch that was reserved for V.I.P. clientele while three strippers danced in front of him. They turned around and waved their asses from side to side, buck naked. All three pussies were shaven bald. He reached out and ran his fingers through the Mexican goddess's pussy lips. She was in the middle of the trio. Out of the three, hers was the meatiest. They felt good to him. "I'm going to have to see what this be like a li'l later on. Ain't that right, Fancii?"

Fancii was so high that she could barely focus. Everything seemed as if it was fuzzy. She had more than two grams of China White in her system. Mills had been feeding her all day long in celebration of his eighteenth birthday. He had her fitted in a five thousand dollar Vera Wang gown that enhanced and complemented her every curve. Her neck was draped with pink diamonds. So was her wrist. She looked expensive and had felt good before she pumped too much dope into her body. She squeezed her eyelids together and opened them. She smiled at Mills as best she could. "That's right, baby. It's your day. Whatever my man wants, he gets."

"You damn right I do, and I want her, and us, in the bed tonight, so that's gon' happen." He pulled the Mexican down into his lap and sucked on her neck. His right hand cupped her breast. "Say, mami, you wanna suck this dick in a mansion?"

She nodded. "Jess. Jess I do," she answered in broken English.

Mills laughed. "Bitch, I bet."

Fancii felt nauseous. She leaned into Mills's ear. "Baby, I'll be right back. I have to go to the bathroom. Do you mind?"

Milos dug his nails into her thighs. He didn't know why he liked to handle her so rough. Maybe it was because he thought he had to overcompensate for the fact he knew she still craved Noodles. He'd knocked him out in front of her, and that still caused him to feel embarrassed. Or maybe it was the fact that he knew she was from the hood. He felt that she was accustomed to being treated as such by the savages back there in Crenshaw. "Fancii, you don't tell me what you're going to do, you ask me."

Fancii wanted to snap out at him. She was beginning to hate the sight of his face, no matter how handsome it was. She so desperately wanted to tell him to go to hell, but she knew she couldn't. She'd already done two photo shoots for Covergirl, and everything was going well. She was able to lay her head in a three-story mansion instead of the ghetto of Crenshaw, and for the most part, she was treated as a Queen and had everything handed to her.

There were just sudden spurts of mistreatment by Mills that caused her to question everything, things that made her want to leave him, but she feared what leaving him looked like. After the people at Covergirl found out that she was familiar with Bronco Banks's son, she'd been getting special privileges ever since. She couldn't go back to the slum life that she'd once known. She was trapped in the clutches of the fame and fortune. "I'm sorry, baby. May I go to the bathroom?"

Mills smiled while the strippers danced in front of him. The music blaring out of the speakers was so loud that he could barely hear himself think. "Yes, you may. But hurry up before they start singing happy birthday to me. I don't want you to miss that."

Fancii rose from the couch and nearly threw up. She took a deep breath and gathered herself. The club was packed. All three stages had feature dancers on them shaking their asses to the music coming out of the speakers. It smelled like weed smoke, cigarettes, perfume, alcohol, and pussy in the air.

Mils grabbed her hand and slid a nickel-sized amount of China White into it. "Go get yourself right, baby, and bring yo' ass back here."

Fancii staggered into the bathroom. Once there, she took a deep breath and exhaled slowly. She looked over her reflection in the mirror. On the surface she looked radiant. Absolutely beautiful. Her jewels caused her natural fineness to pop. Her long hair was curly, jet black, with brunette highlights that offset her red bottoms and skin tone. She smiled at her reflection and wiped her nose, fiending for a fix. She dumped the nickel bag of dip onto the vanity counter, separated it into two lines, and began to toot them. She was working on the second line when the door to the bathroom swung inward.

Cheyenne stepped through with Sky and stopped in her tracks when she saw Fancii tooting the line. At first she thought she was seeing things. She just knew for a fact that her friend wasn't taking part in such a filthy habit. She waited until she lifted her head to say something. "Fancii? Gurl, I know you ain't doing what I think you is?"

Fancii threw her head back and wiped her nose. She dusted the China off of the counter. Her heart beat fast in her chest. She looked over and into the face of Cheyenne, Noodles's older sister. "Girl, what the hell you doing here? I thought you said you was gon' call me if you could make it."

Cheyenne stepped next to her with a frown on her face. "Girl, what the hell were you doing?"

Fancii wiped at her nose. She felt embarrassed. She tried to get her brain together, but her high was fresh. There was a loud song going off in her head. The melody was perfect. Her body felt numb and breezy. Cheyenne looked fuzzy to her. She opened up her mouth to talk, but no sound came out of it.

Sky stepped inside and stood in front of the door. "Girl, when your brother finds out about this, he gon' go crazy. Noodles too. You already know how much he love yo' ass."

Fancii shook her head. "I wasn't doing nothing. Y'all thinking y'all something when you didn't," she lied, standing in front of the sink.

Cheyenne moved her out of the way and ran her finger over the spot of the vanity where Fancii had tooted the drug. After collecting a bit of residue, she put the finger in her mouth. She wanted to see if the drug would numb her tongue or leave a real foul taste indicating that it was something harsh. The latter was the case. Her eyes grew bucked. "H? You're in here doing H? What the fuck is wrong with you, Sis?" She grabbed her by the shoulder. and shook her.

Fancii's heart was pounding in her chest. "I-I-I, was just trying something. I mean, with my mother being killed, and Filipino nearly, dying I've been... I just..." She lowered her head and shook it.

Sky stepped forward. "That's the first thing these rich boys do when they get a sister from the hood. They turn them out in all kinds of drugs. I should have warned you, and that's my fault. The Banks family's children are known for dibbing and dabbing with all types of shit. If I was you, I'd get out quick. Come on, let's go." Sky took ahold of Fancii's wrist.

Fancii yanked it away. "No. I'm grown. I know what the fuck I'm doing. I don't need nobody treating me like a child."

"A child? Girl, I don't know what you're thinking, but I love you. I'm concerned about you. We been the best of friends ever since the third grade. If anybody knows what type of pain you're dealing with, it's me. After all, he is my half-brother. Now let us get you home, and off of that heroin crap." Cheyenne tried to take ahold of her hand.

Fancii imagined driving back to the slums of Crenshaw with them and nearly threw up. She didn't want to go back to roach-infested houses and drive-by shootings. Mills had turned her on to the high life, and there was no way that she couldn't look back now. He was her ticket to a world of glitz and glamour. Ever since the personnel had found out that she was dating Mills Banks, she'd booked three photo shoots and two magazine spreads. She was also set to be the face for a new Rock the Vote campaign in the summer. Things were looking up, and she believed that it was all because of her connection to Mills Banks. She jerked away from

Cheyenne. "Fuck the hood. I don't belong there any-more. I ain't never going back. This is what it is. I'd appreciate if you bitches stay out of my bidness."

"Who you talking to like that, Fancii? You got me fucked up." Sky scrunched her face and made her way in the direction of Fancii.

Cheyenne blocked her path. "Nall, girl, chill. She right. She is grown. Let her do what she gon' do." She turned to Fancii. "Girl, I love you. Whenever you need me, you know how to get ahold of me." She stepped forward and wrapped her arms around her and kissed her cheeks.

"I love you too, and I will." Fancii hugged her back.

Mils busted through the door. He eyed all three girls carefully and curled his upper lip. He wondered what they'd been saying to Fancii. Had Noodles sent them to get her back? Was he missing the model? That tickled him a bit. He stepped to Fancii and took ahold of her hand. "Baby, let's go, they're about to sing happy birth-day. I want you by my side when they do."

As Mills led her out of the bathroom, she took a sec-ond to glance over her shoulder. She looked into the concerned eyes of her friends and felt a bit of remorse for how she'd come down on them. But they represented a place where she never wanted to return. A painful past. Her direction was forward. No matter what she had to do to reach success, she was willing to do it.

Chapter 7

"Bruh, I still can't believe she did that. Why the hell you ain't tape them ankles together or something?" Filipino asked. He cut the French toast with his fork and placed the portion into his mouth, chewing loudly. "That bitch jumped out of the back seat and got to booking so fast that I couldn't catch her. I ain't never seen a female run that fast." He laughed and forked a nice amount of cheese omelet into his mouth.

It was two days after the female was supposed to take them out to Oakland and show them where Combo was ducked off. They were at a restaurant called Good Morning. The small hole in the wall establishment was known for some of the best breakfast food in town.

Noodles took a swallow of his apple juice. "Bruh, that shit over wit'. We slipped. Ain't nobody to blame. Next time we know not to put nobody in the back seat without really making sure they can't get away. It's cool, a lesson learned. We gotta get on to bigger and better thangs. Dwayne say we gotta hit up these two Italian cats that been shaking down his supporter's businesses. They're saying that if they find out that they're donating to his campaign that their stores will be burned to the ground. One of the store owners has already been beaten pretty bad. We gotta put a stop to this shit right away and get in they asses. Plus, bonus, it's in the north side of Los Angeles, so if shit get out of order, we can leave them bodies right where they are." Noodles cut his Tennessee Pride sausage and dumped it into his mouth. It was nice and spicy, just like he liked it.

"So when we supposed to be taking care of that?" Filipino asked, looking around the small restaurant. The

63

place was packed. Smacking and all kinds of conversations could be heard loudly throughout the establishment.

"In two days. I wanna take some time off to chill with my mother and sister, bruh. I think we both understand how short life is. I wanna make sure I remember to appreciate my Queen while she's still here."

Filipino felt sick. A vision of his own mother came across his mind. He missed her. He wished that he could spend time with her one more time. "Bruh, I can feel that. Maybe I'll hit up Fancii so I can see what's good with her. Hopefully she'd like to go out to dinner or something. Ever since she been rocking with your brother she been acting real funny toward me, Noodles. I don't like that shit because we all we got, bruh." Filipino's heart was heavy. He felt so alone outside of Noodles. He wished that his nother was still alive. There was his father back in the Philippines, but their relationship was weak at best. There was no one like his mother.

Noodles saw images of himself killing Mills. First his father had left their family behind to pick up a new family and move all them way out to Bel-Air with an Italian woman, crushing his young heart. Now, many years later, the love of his life was leaving him behind to do the same exact thing. It was defeating. "Bruh, that's your sister. Won't nobody ever know her better than you do. You should be able to get her to spend some time with you. Tell her you miss her. That you need her. Fancii got a good heart. She'll come running."

Filipino shrugged his shoulders. "I don't know about doing all of that, but I will tuck my tail. I do miss her crazy ass."

Noodles missed her as well. He ate the remainder of his food in silence, the entire time reminiscing about the good times he'd had with Fancii. He had to clear his head. "Look, bruh, I'ma fuck wit' you in a few days. I need to be around my Queens. This whole thing wit' Fancii is getting the better of me. I gotta go before I wind up smoking somebody else on the strength of her." He stood up and placed a fifty dollar bill on the table. "That should cover both of our meals. You can leave the tip."

Filipino nodded. "That's cool, Cuz. I'ma chill here for a minute though. Finna hit up Fancii and see if she'll fuck wit' me. Love doe, fool."

"Yep, love, fool," Noodles returned, making his way out of the restaurant.

***

Noodles stood at the foot of the stairs, waiting patiently for his mother Sondra to emerge along with Cheyenne. He was dressed in a black and gray Gucci suit over Rockports. He smelled good and had a fresh haircut. He rocked a gold Movado in his left wright and had two diamond studs in each ear. He felt good. For the night, he didn't want to think about nothing else other than spoiling his Queens.

Sondra was the first to appear at the top of the stairs. The black and red Fendi dress clung to her curves. The matching red bottoms fit perfectly on her small feet. She brushed her curls out of her dark-skinned face and made her way down the flight of stairs, taking them one at a time. "Baby, I ain't felt this good in years." She laughed and continued to descend the stairs.

Noodles opened his arms and allowed for her to walk into them. Once there, he hugged her. He held her for a long while, then kissed her forehead. He took a step back and held her hands out. "Mama, you look good. I mean damn, you bad."

Sondra laughed and turned in a circle for him. "You think so?"

He eyed her up and down. "Definitely."

"Maybe I'ma go out tonight and find you a step-daddy," she joked.

Noodles was smiling, but after hearing that, he frowned with anger written across his face. "Don't play wit' me. You'll get that nigga kilt quick pressing up on my moms." He meant that.

Sondra batted her eyelashes at him. "So, what, I'm just supposed to stay single forever?"

He shook his head. "Nall, not forever, just until I die. Then you can do whatever you want."

She rolled her eyes. "Why thank you. You're too kind."

Cheyenne came to the top of the stairs and cleared her throat. "Noodles, I'm sorry, bro, but I can't go."

"Can't go? Why?" he shot back at her.

"Because I gotta take care of something that's important. I can't get into it right now, but just know that I would never call off a family date night if it wasn't important. I'm sorry though, bro." She came all the way down the stairs, wrapped her arms around his neck, and held her cheek against his.

Noodles was seething. "Damn, Cheyenne, I don't never get a chance to spend no time with y'all. Now the one time that I'm really trying to, you kick me to the curb. That's bogus."

Cheyenne took a step back and held his face in her small hands. "Little brother, I know that you love me. I know that you want for us to spend time together, and we will. Just not tonight. How about tomorrow, or the next day?"

Noodles shrugged his shoulder stubborn-like. "I guess. I done planned all this stuff though. But I guess we'll figure something out on a later date."

Sondra slightly bumped Cheyenne out of the way. "It's okay, Nadell. That just means that you can spend more time catering to me. I ain't got no problem with that." She kissed him. "Let's go, baby."

***

Filipino waited until Noodles's black Eddie Bauer truck pulled down the block. He rolled down the alley and parked in the back of Sondra's house. By the time he made it across the backyard, Cheyenne was already waiting in the back door with a silk purple robe slightly opened, just enough to reveal the black lace lingerie underneath. He stepped into the door frame and picked her up. She wrapped her thick thighs around his waist, and they began to make out. Filipino kicked the door closed and carried her into the house with pussy on his mind.

Combo watched the scene from two yards over. He lowered the binoculars and shook his head. He tapped the shoulder of the hitta next to him. "Cuz, I bet you any money that that back door open. What you wanna bet?" he asked him.

The hitta pulled a Glock out of his waistband. "So, what you saying? We about to fuck them over or what?" He stood up with the black ski mask over his face.

Combo placed a finger to his mask. "Hush, nigga. Let me run this show. We gon' let that nigga fuck for a li'l while, then we gon' try the back door. If that bitch locked it, we gon' drench the crib with gasoline and burn that ma'fucka to the ground. It's as simple as that." The hitta nodded his head. "It's yo' world, Combo. Long as they wind up on the news, it's all good to me." Combo patted him on the back. "I like how you think, boy. That's why I fuck with you. Come on, let's go and get the gasoline just in case." Combo watched the house for a few seconds longer, and then they jogged back to his van to retrieve the gas can.

***

Sondra looked around the fancy restaurant. She was amazed. This had been the first time in a long time that she'd stepped outside of Crenshaw. They were in SoHo, an upscale part of Los Angeles. The restaurant was five star all across the board. Their truck had been valeted. There was light jazz playing in the background. The waiters were dressed in tuxedos. They spoke to them respectfully and walked around with white cloths draped over their arms. Noodles had three candles burning on their table. The restaurant was nice and dimly lit. The ambiance was comfortable. Sondra looked across the table at Noodles and smiled. "It's lovely, baby."

He poured more Moët into his glass and filled hers. "Mama, you are a Queen. If I don't treat you as such, you just might lose sight of that fact, and we can't allow that to happen. You been struggling since day one. Never took days off from being an incredible mother. I just wanna let you know that I appreciate you, and you mean the world to me. Huh, Queen." He slid her a jewelry box across the table that encased a diamond tennis bracelet with yellow diamonds. Even in the dimly lit restaurant, the diamonds sparkled.

Sondra's eyes were misty. "Oh my God, baby, it's beautiful. It looks so, so good. You've outdone yourself with this." She got up from her seat and planted kisses all over his face. "I love you. I love you. I love you. You're the best son in the whole wide world."

Noodles blushed and sat her back in her seat. "Mama, that's not it. I wanna move you out of Crenshaw for good."

"Out of Crenshaw? Baby, where you get the money to do that?" she wondered and became afraid at the same time.

"I don't want you worrying about all of that. I just need you to start putting stuff in boxes. I'm serious, I'm getting you the hell out of there. You're my life, and you deserve the best." He took ahold of her wrist and placed the bracelet upon her right one.

She held it up and looked it over. She immediately became emotional. No man had ever done even half as much as Noodles had done for her. That was ridiculous. He was her son. "Baby, I don't want you thinking about moving me out of no hood. You should be focused on going to college. Bettering yourself. That way you could move us out of the ghetto legally. That street life will always come back to haunt you. Look at what happened to Filipino and his mother. If you play around in the devil's backyard, he makes the rules. The only path of righteousness is following the path of Jesus Christ. If there was one thing that I wanted to instill in my children, it was that." She lowered her head. "Guess I screwed that up though."

Noodles didn't know what to say. He held his silence until after they ordered off of the menu. He took a swallow from his Moët and took ahold of her hand. "Mama, every lesson that you instilled in me regarding Jehovah resonated. I know who he is, trust and believe that. But it's like you said, that devil is real also. I'm out here every day warring with his minions. My heart is cold, not because of what you failed to teach me, but because of our environment. Its kill or be killed out there, Mama, and your son chooses to kill rather than to be killed. As long as we living in Crenshaw, it's gon' be that way. That's why I gotta get us out of there. So, when you get home, you start getting pack. That's that. I love you, and it's my job to make sure that you and my sister are straight at all times. I'ma keep doing that by any means until there is no more breath in my body. I owe you everything that I am as a man. A mother is the title of a Goddess that should be worshipped. Period. You hear me?"

Sondra didn't know what to say, so she simply nodded.

***

Combo was on the second gas can. He and his hitta had doused all along the sides of the house. They even poured some on the grass, along the windowsill, and all over the porch. He was actually happy that Filipino had locked the back door. He had an image of him roasting in a fire inside of his mind and that brought him great pleasure. After the can was empty, he jogged back to his van and set it inside of it. He searched his pocket until he found a lighter. His smile broadened.

"Let's see you escape this shit, Mr. Invincible," he mused out loud.

Hood Rich

Chapter 8

Cheyenne pulled Filipino's shirt over his head and pushed him into the wall. Her lips were pressed against his swiftly, kissing, licking, and sucking. She moaned into his mouth.

Filipino's hands slid over her hips, around and back, until he was cuffing her ass. The cheeks were soft and warm. He kneaded them like fresh dough. "I been thinking about this pussy all day, Cheyenne. When I'm feeling like I'm feeling, you the only one that can take me away from this shit. I need you, shawty." He sucked on her neck and bit into it with his teeth. He scraped them across the vein in her neck.

Cheyenne purred and humped into him. She took a step back and dropped her robe completely. She grabbed the remote control from the dresser and activated the music. Trey Songs's "Jupiter Love" resonated from the speakers. She stepped up on to the bed and stood in the middle of it. She looked into his slanted eyes and smiled. "I need you too, Filipino. You know you got this on lock."

Her body began to move to the beat of the melody. Slowly, her hips started to wind like a snake. She turned around and showcased the fact that her G-string separated her dark brown cheeks before turning all the way back around and facing him. Her small hand ran over her stomach, all the way down to her sex lips. She played over them through the thin, transparent material. "You want me, daddy? Huh?"

Filipino had already undressed down to his boxers. His piece throbbed, jerking time and again. His eyes devoured her body. She was thick, the sexiest shade of chocolate in the world, he believed, and from experience, he knew that she tasted just as sweet. He felt some type of way when it came to their relationship because it was the only secret that he'd ever kept from Noodles. Noodles knew that he was a player, that he loved pussy. His only wishes were that he stayed away from Cheyenne.

Noodles knew how hard his sister loved and didn't want her to get caught up with a dude like Filipino because he was a male whore. Noodles had told Filipino time and time again after Cheyenne had expressed her like of Filipino that he never wanted Filipino to cross those lines, and Filipino had agreed. But over the years, Cheyenne became finer and finer, and thicker. She was a Jamaican goddess. His infatuation of her had risen through the roof, and three summers ago, they started to creep like TLC. He nodded his head up at her. "Hell yeah, daddy ready, baby. I'm ready right now. Come here."

She stepped to the edge of the bed. He reached up and rubbed the front of her panties. The lips were plump. The fabric seemed moist. He licked the juices off of his fingers, looking into her eyes.

Cheyenne opened her thighs a little further and grabbed the back of his head. She thrust her mound into his face. "Eat me, daddy. Taste me right now," she moaned.

Filipino licked the fabric that encased her treasures. He placed his nose right on her fold and sniffed her chocolate delights. She smelled good to him, like a shot of pussy that was off limits. He yanked her panties to the side and licked up and down her crease. His tongue invaded her pink, and then he was sucking on her clit that protruded from the top of her hood while two of his fingers slipped inside of her playground.

"Uhhhhhhhh! Shit, Filipino!" she moaned, crouching down just enough to take his thrusting fingers.

Filipino moved them in and out faster and faster. Her pussy juices seeped out of her and ran down her thick thighs. Filipino licked up her spills. He pushed her backward and climbed on the bed. Then he picked her up and slammed her down. He forced her knees to her chest before he was orally making love to her box, sucking and licking all over the folds before he spread the lips wide and focused solely on her clitoris.

Cheyenne held her pussy open for him. She bucked her eyes as he ate her with reckless abandon. His tongue was a blur. It sent shivers through her. Every time he nipped at her bud, she jerked with pleasure. It felt so good that she wanted to tell him how much she loved his fine ass. Instead, she chose to communicate through moans. "Mmm. Mmm. Filipino. Daddy. Daddy. Mmm. Shit. I can't. I can't. Take it." She arched her back and grabbed ahold of her breasts, squeezing them. The long nipples poked through her fingers.

Filipino fingered her pussy faster and faster. "Cum for daddy, baby. Cum for me. I wanna taste you." Faster and faster, he sucked in her clit as firmly as he could. His tongue went back and forth across it, and then he was sucking again, swallowing her juices.

"Uhhhhh. Uhhhhhhhh. I'm cumming. I'm cumming. Oh fuck!" Cheyenne hollered before falling back on the bed, shaking as her orgasm rocked her body violently.

Filipino saw her skeet at him. Her pussy spit twice, and then began to leak like a broke faucet. His tongue licked at her secretions. He slurped them and continued to play in her box. His fingers were slimy wet. He pulled them out and sucked them into his mouth. "Damn, baby. You taste so good. You so sweet. You gon' give me cavities."

Cheyenne kicked her legs out and pulled him down, flipped him on his back, and pumped his piece in her fist after removing his boxers. "Two can play this game." She licked around his head and sucked only the tip into her mouth.

Filipino's eyes rolled into the back of his head. "Shit, baby. That's why I love yo' ass. You something else," he groaned.

Cheyenne popped his dick out. "I love you too, Filipino. That goes without saying." Cheyenne swallowed her spit. She sucked him into her mouth and went to work on him. She deep throated like a veteran, adding a bunch of spit only to slurp it back up. Then her head was spearing in his lap.

Filipino whimpered. He humped into her mouth over and over. His abs tightened. His fingers roamed through her hair while she pleased him. There was something about Cheyenne that drove him crazy. Whenever he felt alone, he sought her, and the feeling had a way of disappearing. He pushed her off of him. "Baby, I want some of this pussy. Get yo' ass up here right now and put that Jamaican shit on me. You go first, because when it's my turn, we gon' fuck fa real." He laid back and stroked his dick, awaiting her mounting.

Cheyenne felt her pussy quiver as she took up the position. She straddled his waist and reached under her. She took ahold of his long, thick penis. She ran the big head up and down her crease before planting it on her hole and easing down on it. Her eyes rolled into the back of her head as she engulfed him.

Filipino felt the heat and groaned. She was so wet that her cream was already spilling over onto his balls. It felt like he'd entered into a swampy cave that squeezed him like a fist. "Ride me, baby. Ride me. Now." He gripped her fat ass and dug his fingers into her flesh.

Cheyenne arched her back and popped forward. She popped backward and forward again, then repeated the process, taking him deep into her kitty. She leaned down and sucked his neck. "Un. Un. Un. Filipino. Daddy. I love you. Oooh. Fuck. Fuck. I love you, daddy. Un. Un. Yes. Yes." Her hips rotated in a circular motion. She rode him faster and faster. "Aw. Aw. Daddy."

He threw his head back and groaned deep within his throat. "Ride this dick. Ride this dick. Fuck me, Cheyenne. Damn, baby. Fuck."

She sped up the pace. The bed began to go haywire. The headboard knocked into the wall over and over again. The springs squeaked. Her shoulder straps fell off of her arms, exposing her chocolate breasts. Her nipples were so hard that they stood up an inch from the areolas.

Filipino pulled her down enough to suck on them one at a time. He squeezed her pretty titties together and licked all over them, humping up from the bed to plant his dick as far into her as it would go. It felt so glorious to him. He felt her tightened her walls and could no longer hold back. "I'm cumming, Cheyenne. I'm cumming, baby."

She slammed down on his piece, over and over, milking him. She felt his nut shoot up and tap her walls. She shook and squeezed her eyelids together. The feeling of the invasion was almost too much for her. His warm seed filled her and spilled downward along his length.

Filipino flipped her over and continued to slowly work his dick in and out of her. It didn't take long before it was hard as a rock again. He threw her thighs on his shoulders and proceeded to plunge into her box as hard as he could, fucking that pussy like a beast, while she played with her nipples and moaned with her mouth wide open.

***

Combo took the newspaper and set it ablaze. He dropped it on the line of gasoline and watched it follow the trail leading to Sondra's house. In seconds, the house was on fire. He squeezed the bottle of lighter fluid to enhance the flames. Then he stood back and laughed.

His hitta lit the porch on fire and jumped off of it. He squeezed his bottle of lighter fluid all along the side of the house and took off running toward the back of it, constantly looking over his shoulder as the flames got bigger and bigger.

***

Filipino pulled Cheyenne up by her hair and fucked her hard from the back. Her juicy ass cheeks crashed into his lap. They jiggled, along with her thighs. He watched his dick go in and out of her. The sight was enough to drive him crazy. "Damn, this pussy good, Cheyenne. This pussy good. I'm finna cum again. I'm finna cum again. Argh, fuck!"

Cheyenne bounced back harder and harder. Her nut was close. She could feel it. She diddled her clitoris. Pinched it. A ripple went through her and then she was cumming with him. "Uhhhhhhhh shit. I'm cumming, Filipino. I'm. Cumming!" she screamed.

Filipino came hard and fell on top of her. His dick twitching inside of her.

Then he smelt it. Clear as day. Smoke. He sniffed the air.

Cheyenne smelt it at the same time he did. She sniffed the air, and thought she was bugging. "Daddy, you smell that?"

Filipino pulled out and jumped out of the bed. Now he knew he wasn't tripping. "Hell yeah, it smells like smoke."

"Nall, more like burnt wood." He rushed to the bedroom window and looked out of it. The sight of the fire on the house almost gave him a heart attack. "Oh shit, the house on fire."

Cheyenne jumped out of the bed and threw on her panties. "On fire? How the hell is it on fire?" She threw on a pair of pants. She went for her Air Max's just as the glass table downstairs shattered. The room got hot. It felt like they were in an oven.

Filipino threw on his pants, grabbed the knob of the bedroom door, and burned himself. "Aww fuck!"

"What?" Cheyenne was terrified.

He ripped the sheet off of the bed and used it to turn the knob. As soon as he pulled open the door, a rush of fire spilled into the room, knocking him backward on to his ass.

Cheyenne screamed. "Oh my God!" The smoke began to choke her. Thick black clouds of it. She covered her face and tried her best to breathe only when she had to, but it was no use. Every time she inhaled, she started to choke. "Filipino!"

He got to his feet, coughing. The flames spread across the carpet and engulfed the sheets on the bed. Filipino rushed and grabbed Cheyenne's hand. "Baby, come on. We gotta get out of here."

The song stopped playing. The radio exploded. Cheyenne started to panic. She looked out of the room door and saw that the hallway was fully engulfed. Tears streamed down her face. Smoke traveled up her nose, choking her worse than before. This ignited her asthma. She could no longer breathe. She grabbed her throat and fell to the floor. The fire scorched her back and the side of her right shoulder, peeling her skin away from her body.

"Cheyenne!" Filipino hollered with the smoke burning his eyes. He couldn't see. With every breath he inhaled a thick cloud of black smoke. He coughed and looked around the heavily foggy room. "Cheyenne!"

***

Combo took the Mach Ninety and slammed the hundred round clip into it. He stood beside his hitta and mugged the house. "Chop this bitch down. Shoot!"

Boom. Boom. Boom. Boom. Boom.

They bucked at the house, adding gunfire to the already chaotic display. Combo watched the windows shatter and big chunks of wood pop off of the house. He laughed loudly and continued to bust. "This that war shit right here. This how you get at a nigga's ass." *Boom. Boom. Boom.* He busted as his hitta did the same.

***

"So, did you enjoy yourself, Mama?" Noodles asked Sondra as they took the exit off of the highway and pulled to a halt at the red lights.

"I absolutely did, baby. You outdid yourself. I ain't gon' forget about this day ever. It felt good to spend some time with my baby boy. I love you, baby, and I hope we got an understanding." She smiled at him.

Noodles rested his right hand in the steering wheel. "Long as that understanding is that when you get home you'll pack your things, then yeah, we have one." The light flashed green. He stepped on the gas and accelerated toward their street. His eyes caught sight of the big cloud of smoke that had risen from his mother's duplex, though where the smoke emanated from was unbeknownst to him.

Sondra reached over and took a hold of his hand. "Boy, what am I going to do with you? You just gon' make me move, huh?"

He nodded. "You dang ol' right."

Sondra laughed and sat back in her seat. "Well, I guess that's that then."

Noodles was a block away from their place of residence. Now there was smoke high in the air, and he could smell the scent of burnt wood and hear the sounds of Fire truck, Paramedics, and Police sirens. When he came to their block, it was barricaded by two police officers. He parked and struggled to look down their street.

"What the hell is going on down there?" Sondra asked him out loud.

Noodles jumped out of the truck and slammed the door. He eased into the nosy crowd that had developed outside of the barricade. He searched for a face that looked somewhat familiar to him. He spotted a young teenage boy and stepped to him. "Say, Cuz, what's good? Who shit on fire?"

The teenager looked up at him and recognized his face. "Damn, Noodles, that's your mother's shit, Cuz. Somebody set y'all shit on fire and shot that bitch up. Homie, it's like they was shooting for a long time too."

Noodles heart sank to the pits of his stomach. He felt sick. His eyes for bucked. He rushed toward the barricade. "Say, man, that's my house. That house. My big sister was in there," he hollered, trying to force his way through.

Sondra got out of the truck. "Nadell, what's wrong, baby?" She was worried and feeling sick. Noodles was acting erratic.

The police officer tried to block Noodles from stepping past the barricade, but it was of no use. With a spin to his right, Noodles evaded one police officer and pushed the other. He took off running to his mother's residence. He was two houses away when he started to feel the heat caused by the destruction. "Cheyenne! Cheyenne! Sis, where are you?" he hollered.

Chapter 9
Three weeks later...

Noodles stepped into Cheyenne's hospital room and up to her bed. Cheyenne laid on her back, watching the television screen. Half of her face was covered by a medical gauze.

During the fire, the right side of her face and shoulder had sustained second degree burns. The medical team had done more than ten skin grafts to get her back to as normal as possible. Noodles took ahold of her hand and kissed the back of it. "How you doing, Sis?" He brushed her hair out of her face, then trailed his fingers down her soft cheek.

Cheyenne's throat was dry. Not only was she still in serious pain, but her depression was getting the better of her. If that wasn't enough, during the whole fiasco, she found out that she was two months pregnant with Filipino's child. She had yet to tell him - or anybody else, for that matter. "Noodles, the left side of my face is going to be scarred up for the rest of my life, and so will my shoulder. I'm screwed. I can kiss any hopes of modeling goodbye. I hate this." She closed her eyes and fought back tears, but they wound up coming anyway. They leaked out of her lids and slid into her ear canals.

Noodles wiped them away. His heart was heavy. He rubbed her right cheek. "Sis, you have to be thankful that you are alive. If Filipino hadn't got you out when he did, you could have died. The doctors said you were suffering from intense smoke inhalation, that if you would have stayed in that house for another sixty seconds, you would have choked to death or your lungs would have given up on you." He kissed her cheek. "I'm just thankful you're still with us." He couldn't help but to kiss her forehead again. He loved his sister with all of him. He'd sworn to protect her for the rest of his life when he was only five years old. He felt like a massive failure. He picked up her hand again.

Cheyenne choked back tears. "Noodles, why do we have to go through things like this? Why does it seem like the world is designed for us to fail, and to be hurt in the process? It's just not fair. No part of it is fair."

Noodles teared up. A piece of Cheyenne's bandage was coming loose. He could see the pinkness of her injury with a slight trace of blood. It made him want to break down to his knees. He felt so weak and defeated. He carefully fixed it back, then kissed the back of her hand again. A sole tear slid down his cheeks in empathy for his older sister. "Cheyenne, I don't know why there are so many odds stacked against us, but we are fighters. We can be knocked down a thousand times, but we'll get back up and keep on fighting each time. This is what you have to do right now. You gotta keep on fighting, Sis. I swear I got your back. I'll hold you up."

Cheyenne was silent for a while. Her eyes focused on a crack in the ceiling of the hospital room. Life had always been so hard for her. For them. Ever since they'd left Jamaica, it had been one struggle after the next, one obstacle to overcome after the next. Then there was also the crushing dilemma with her father. The way the man had taken advantage of her as an early teen on more than one of his drunken nights. Besides the scars she'd obtained from the fire, she still lived with those inflicted by the man. "Noodles, I'm pregnant."

Noodles stood frozen. He held her hand, blinking furiously. "Pregnant, by who?" he asked, wondering why whoever the dude was that had gotten her pregnant wasn't there to stand by her side during this rough and vulnerable period.

"I want you to remember that I am older than you. That I can take care of myself, and I don't want you treating me like a fucking little girl. You get that? I'm lying in a fuckin' hospital bed because your enemies chose to attack our home because of some shit you did to them, not me. So, what I'm about to tell you better not escalate into an argument, or any form of verbal fight. Okay?"

Noodles sighed. "Okay."

Cheyenne tried her best to sit up in bed. She winced in pain. Noodles rushed to her side to assist her. She smacked his hand away. "I got it. I'll be okay." She situated herself. Her face began to burn on the left side. She wanted to cry. Hated feeling so weak. She took a deep breath and fought back tears for the second time that evening. She built up the confidence to reveal her secret. "Okay, Noodles, the baby belongs to - "

Filipino rushed into the room. He flew past Noodles and to Cheyenne's bedside. He took ahold of her hand and kissed all over the back of it. "Baby, baby, baby. You're finally up. Damn, you scared the shit out of me. I don't know what I'd do if I lost you, Cheyenne."

Cheyenne's heart was warmed. She softened, and then looked across the room and into Noodles's eyes. He mugged her angrily. She didn't know what to say.

Filipino turned around and saw Noodles. He didn't know when Noodles had gotten there. He straightened and stood up. "Bruh, I should have told you what was good, but you would have been on some funny shit with me and her. Bruh, I care about her. Nall, damn that care talk. I love this woman, man. This who I wanna be with."

Noodles was furious. "You love her? Nigga, how the hell you love my sister when you know what we out there doing in the streets every single day?"

Filipino tried to calm himself down. He knew that Noodles was simply flailing because of being blindsided by his and Cheyenne's relationship. He didn't want to get into any arguments with him. Both men had lethal tempers. He kept that fact at the forefront of his brain.

"Noodles, what did I just tell you before he came into this room? Didn't I tell you that I'm grown? That I can make my own decisions?" Cheyenne snapped.

"Baby, chill, let me get an understanding with your brother. He just - " Filipino started.

"He just nothing," Cheyenne interrupted him. "This is my business. I'm a grown-ass woman and have been for a long time."

"I don't give a fuck about none of that. You still my sister, and it's my job to protect and watch out for you. I been doing that ever since I was a boy." Noodles felt himself become heated.

"And look where the fuck it got me, Noodles? I'm lying in a hospital bed with half of my face burned off. For the rest of my life, people are going to be staring and pointing at me as if I am some sort of freak. So, don't tell me what you've been doing. Clearly you failed." Cheyenne felt a stinging pain in her shoulder. She ignored it. She knew that she had to stand toe to toe with Noodles. She felt that he was always trying to rule the women in his household as if they were his females or something. Cheyenne loved her brother, but she hated the controlling nature that he possessed.

86

Instead of going at Cheyenne, Noodles decided to step into Filipino's face. "Nigga, this all your fault. I told you to stay the fuck away from my sister. Had you done that, she wouldn't have been in this fucked-up position."

Filipino held his silence. Internally he was boiling, but he refused to give Noodles the fight he was looking for. "Say, bruh, I ain't gon' take it there wit' you. I apologize for not hollering at you before her and I started messing around, but on some genuine shit, I love that woman, bruh. It ain't a perfect love on my end yet, but it'll get there." He looked over to Cheyenne. He wanted to snatch her up so bad and hold her. It felt like an eternity since he'd gotten the chance to do that.

Noodles clenched his jaw. He was too angry to think logically. When he looked into Filipino's eyes, all he saw was betrayal. A snake. A homie that had gone behind his back to fuck with someone dear to his heart. In his mind, it was a double cross. He continued to mug Filipino.

"Damn, don't he get some credit for saving my life? Had he not pulled me out of that fire, I would have fried. I owe this man my life, at the very least, so instead of trying to kick off a bunch of unnecessary bullshit, you could thank him for that," Cheyenne spat.

Those words were like a dagger into Noodles's heart. He felt like Filipino had completely turned his sister against him. His temper got the better of him. "You know, it's good. I don't give a fuck what y'all do. Just don't come running to me when this nigga break yo' heart. I been knowing bruh all my life, and he ain't never been able to stick to one piece of pussy. It ain't finna be no different now. But like I said, it's good. Y'all do y'all, leave me out of that shit. Filipino, on some real shit, nigga you already know what it is. When it's all said and done, you gon' have to holler at me with them knuckles. No matter what she talking about, you still betrayed me, homeboy. I gotta take a good look at you for that."

"Wasn't you fuckin wit' Fancii before our half-brother took her from you, and got her hooked on that shit?" Cheyenne asked, clapping back at him. She hoped the realization of what was going on between Mills and Fancii would cause him to redirect his focus.

Noodles snapped his head back. "Got her hooked on what shit?" He perked up.

"Answer the question, Noodles, were you or were you not messing with Fancii? Filipino's sister?"

"You know I was," he retorted angrily.

"Then why is me and Filipino doing our thing such a fuckin problem?" she screamed.

Filipino tried his best to console her. "Baby, chill, you're just adding fuel to the fire. Me and the homie got some things we need to work out, that's all. It's good."

"I didn't go behind his back to fuck with her. Cuz knew out the gate. Whereas when it comes to you, I specifically forbade him from sniffing around you. Now he got you pregnant. That's some bullshit."

"Pregnant?" Filipino gasped, shocked.

"You can't forbid no man from messing wit' me. I'm older than you. Noodles, I swear to God you need to work on your boundary issues. You treating me like I'm your bitch instead of your sister. I'm tired of it. Matter fact, I need you to leave so I can explain to Filipino what I just found out. Thank you for blurting my bidness out too. Ugh." She mugged him.

Noodles sucked his teeth and mugged the pair. "I ain't leaving until you tell me what's going on with Fancii. What do you mean Mills got her hooked on something? Something like what?"

"If she wants you to know, she'll tell you. Simply put, it ain't my business. Now leave." She pointed toward the door.

Noodles stood in disbelief. Filipino avoided eye contact with him. Now wasn't the time to have a pissing war. Cheyenne was right, she and Filipino needed to talk about their future. They needed to decide what they were going to do, for the child's sake. "A'ight, cool. Filipino, I'll catch up wit' you. Y'all go on 'head and hash out everythang. I'm finna see what's good wit' Fancii."

"Good luck; she ain't returning my calls." Those were the last words Filipino said before Noodles disappeared out of the door and closed it. He shook his head. "Damn, we gon' be beefing for a minute over this. Anyway though." He looked down on Cheyenne. "How many months are you, baby?"

"Two."

"And what are you thinking?" he wanted to know.

"I don't know. I wanted to discuss things with you before I decided all of that. Are you ready to be a father?" She looked him over closely.

"That don't matter. Even if I wasn't, I'ma be ready before our baby gets here. I know what I gotta do, and I'm down to do them. Like I said in front of Noodles, I love you, and I wanna have your back. The one thing this fire has done is let me know that I actually am crazy about you, Cheyenne, so we gon' sit in this room for as long as it takes until we get an understanding about our future. You hear me, beautiful?" He kissed her forehead.

She smiled. "Yeah, baby, I do, and it sounds so good."

Chapter 10

Fancii splashed the sink water into her face and took a deep breath. She looked into the mirror with red eyes. Her hair was disheveled. There were slight bags under her eyes. She felt as if she was dying of hunger, and her head hurt.

Mills came from behind her and kissed her cheek. "Good morning, gorgeous. You ready for your photo shoot today?" He moved her long hair out of her face and sucked on her neck.

She pushed back into him. "Wait a minute, baby. Get off of me. You should know that you can't put any passion marks on me. The last time you sent me for a photo shoot like that, the client gave me a hard time. Think, baby." She shook her head and walked around him and back into the connecting bedroom. She opened the massive closet door and searched through it for the appropriate attire for the day. Mills had previously gone nuts with her wardrobe. She had all of the latest clothing designers. She felt good to have such a selection after previously being restricted to just six outfits in the past. She was thinking something by Fendi. She continued to move the hangers with clothes from side to side until her eyes fell on a blue and gray dress by Fendi. She smiled. "Yeah, I'm rocking you today."

Mills came behind her again and grabbed a handful of her hair. He pulled on the strands so hard that she yelped in pain. "Fancii, I see we still having a problem when it comes to our communications."

Her head was jerked backward. "What are you talking about, Mills?"

He pulled harder on her hair. "You know what I'm talking about. What the fuck did you just say in that bathroom back there? Huh?" he hollered through clenched teeth.

Fancii searched her mind. She couldn't think of anything that she could have said that might have pissed him off. She knew to be careful when speaking around him. He had a bad temper. Everything seemed to affect him for the worst one way or the other. She felt him yank harder on her hair. It felt like it was being pulled out by the roots. "Ow! Baby, please just tell me."

"Bitch, don't you ever tell me what I can't do to you. You are my woman. I made you. You belong to me. Get that shit through your head. Okay!"

"Yes!" she hollered.

Mills pushed her on to the bed. "Damn, it seems like you need me to get into yo' ass. You supposed to be thanking me. I been all over town getting you booked for one modeling gig after the next. Calling in favors, and all types of shit. This is the thanks I get? Huh?" He sat on the bed and pulled out a Ziploc bag filled with China. He grabbed a spoon off of the nightstand and dumped a nice portion onto the silver platter that set next to the lamp. Then he created four lines.

Fancii's body began to hurt. She got dizzy at the sight of the product. She needed a wake me up. She was yearning for the poison. She crawled across the bed and slid her hand over Mills's shoulder. "Baby, I'm sorry. You know I didn't mean nothing by it. I know that you take good care of me. You have since day one. Is there any way that I can make my transgression up to you?" she asked, willing to do whatever it took to get a fix. She squeezed his penis through his pajama pants, then snuck her hand inside so she could pull it out.

Mills laid back. "Seem like you're already reading my mind." He tooted a line hard and coughed. He picked up the bottled water and drank half of it.

Fancii sucked him into her mouth. She held him in her fist and pumped him while she deep throated his pipe. Her tongue played over his helmet while she bobbed her head up and down.

Mills reached across her back and rubbed all over her ass. He pulled the short, silk, Victoria's Secret nightgown upward, exposing her naked pussy. His fingers played over the lips. He felt her dew, then two of his digits slid into her hot pocket.

"Unnnn. Mills." More sucking. She opened her eyes and focused on the platter of China. She yearned for a taste. Needed it. She imagined what the powdery substance would do to her body, and nearly came. She had to get Mills off. Every time he came, he made sure that he gave her a fix. She popped his dick out and stroked it fast. "Cum for me, Mills. Cum for me, baby. Please." She sucked him back in and added more spit. She slurped and tugged away on his manhood.

The drug coursed through Mills and heightened his senses. Everything that she did felt good. All of it. He fingered her faster and faster. He played in her pussy. He could feel her become more and more wet. "Aw fuck, Fancii. Fuck, baby." He grabbed the back of her head and forced her to take more of him.

Fancii gagged and opened her mouth wider. She held him at the base and proceeded to suck him harder and faster. His balls rose too. They became tight. She knew that that usually signified that he was on the verge of cumming. She pumped faster and sucked harder and slid her tongue into his pee hole.

That did it for Mills. He jerked and growled. He tightened his fingers in her hairs and came hard. "Uh. Uh. Uh. Shit, Fancii. Fuck," he groaned, shaking.

She sucked harder and swallowed his seed. She closed her eyes tighter and imagined sitting in front of the platter and having her taste of heaven. That caused her to shiver.

Mills pulled his fingers out of her and sucked them into his mouth. He handed her the platter of China. "Here, baby, party. Party, and then let's go and get this money."

Fancii nearly broke her neck obtaining it. She jumped out of the bed and set the platter on the floor. She laid on her stomach and took one line to the head hard while pinching a nostril. She allowed for the dug to take its effect, and then she was doing the same thing with her other nostril.

Mills stood over her, stroking his piece. His eyes were on her rounded ass. He could see a hint of her bald pussy lips. The sight drove him crazy. He laughed to himself. He loved the power he had over her. She belonged to him, and there was nothing anybody could do about it, not even his brother Noodles. As long as he kept the China coming, Fancii was his property. It was a power he could get used to.

***

Eliza held her lap top on her lap and smiled. "Sir, you're surging in the polls. You are literally only three points behind Mayor Haynes now. I think after your speech today, and the Boys and Girls club openings for the south side this Saturday, you'll be able to go ahead. How do you feel?" she asked him as the limousine traveled through downtown Los Angeles.

Bronco shrugged his shoulders and took a sip from his Vitamin water. "I think it's looking better, but we still have a lot of work to do. You should meet with your contacts once again and tell them to turn up the heat. The crime wave has to intensify. There should be a surge after my speech detailing how I am going to curb the crime in our city, and how Mayor Haynes has forgotten about the people. I want them to become his enemies. To see me as a savior. Oh, it's going to be sweet, don't you think?"

Eliza crossed her thighs. Her Prada skirt moved backward on her legs. "Mr. Banks, I think it sounds awesome, and it's going to be sweet. Let me make a few calls so we can build off of this momentum. You get ready for your speech. Leave the rest to me." She pulled out her cell phone and dialed Combo.

* * *

Noodles pulled the mask over his face and waited until Mills got out of the truck, then walked inside the gas station. He'd been following behind him and Fancii for nearly an hour. He was thankful that they had finally stopped. As soon as the doors closed, he ran from the side of the gas station and rushed to the driver's side of Mills's black Range Rover. He pulled open the door and jumped behind the wheel, throwing it in drive.

"Ahhhhh! Ahhhhh! Let me out of here! Let me out of here! You can have the truck!" she screamed. She tried to pull on the handle of the door, but Noodles locked it from his side.

Noodles flew past the lights of the busy intersection and turned onto a residential street before finding and storming down the alley. When he got to the middle of it, he slammed on the brakes and backed it into a garage. After he parked the truck, he killed the ignition and pulled his mask off.

Before she could tell that it was Noodles, Fancii rushed across the center and flooded Noodles with fist after fist. "Let me go! Let me go! Let me go!" she screamed with her eyes closed.

Noodles allowed her to punch him more than ten times, then he threw her to the floor of the truck and pulled his mask off. "Fancii. Fancii. Baby, it's me. Calm yo' ass down." He grabbed ahold of her wrists and pinned them to the floor.

Fancii hesitated to open her eyes. When she did, she looked into his face with anger. "Noodles! What the fuck have you done?" she screamed. "Let me up. Let me up right now. We gotta go back and get Mills."

He winced. "What?" His heart hurt.

"Let me go. I'm not playing wit' you." She tried to kick up at him.

He straddled her waist and held her steady. "Fuck Mills. What's this shit I hear about him getting you hooked on some fuckin drug? Huh? What the fuck this nigga got you hooked on?"

Fancii shook her head from right to left. "Let me up, Noodles. It ain't your fuckin' business. Let me go. I gotta go find him before he leaves me in the hood. Get the fuck off of me."

Noodles held her more firmly. He looked into her eyes. Even beyond the makeup, he could see the bags beneath her eyes. She appeared skinnier. Her face was slightly sunken from the last time he'd seen her. There was definitely a change. This wasn't the woman he'd grown up from a little kid with. "Fancii, please talk to me, baby. Tell me what's going on. I love you. I still love you."

Fancii was high as a kite. Noodles was ruining it for her. She began to panic. She would lose her kind if Mills gave up on her, if he left her in the hood or stripped her from the privilege that being on his arm had presented her. She loved him, but he represented nothing but struggle and pain. He represented the ghetto, a life that she so desperately wanted to leave behind "Noodles, I don't love you anymore. I've moved on. You need to do the same thing. Please get off of me so I can go back to my man."

Noodles shook his head. "Fancii, don't say that shit to me. It's always been us. Just me and you. Please don't fuck that off now."

Fancii mugged him. "Noodles, I swear to God, get the fuck off of me! You're acting like a fatal attraction. Now I'm done fuckin' with you. That's what it is!"

Noodles sat back. "So that's what it's gon' be, huh? You gon' choose Mills over me? After all we've been through?"

She pushed him hard and slid from under him. "You can't offer me shit, Noodles. We ain't been through nothing but heartache and pain ever since we were children. I'm tired of it. I aspire for something better. I refuse to go out like my mother did. I have to be better for myself first, and then my mother. I promised her a brighter future, and it sucked that I couldn't deliver. You and Filipino cut her life short. I'll never forgive either one of you for that." She got up and behind the wheel of the truck. "Bye, Noodles. Never contact me again. I officially hate you, and my brother."

Noodles was at a loss for words. He kept his silence and jumped out of the truck. He stood there in the alley as Fancii stormed away. The wheels burned rubber, kicking rocks into the air, and then she was gone. He lowered his head, crushed. Tears ran down his cheeks. "First my sister turned her back on me. Then my right-hand man betrayed me. Now my first love done shit on me for my half-brother. A'ight. It's all good." He nodded his head, his heart turning into a block of ice.

***

Fancii pulled the truck in front of Mills as he was on the phone with the local authorities. She slammed on the brakes and opened the passenger's door. "Baby, it was that dumb-ass nigga Noodles. He trying to get me back."

Mills got into the truck and slammed the door. He reached across the aisle and slapped her so hard that she spit across the windshield. He grabbed her by the neck and flung her to the floor, slapping her over and over. "I'm. Tired. Of. You. Playin'. These. Games. Wit'. Me. You. And. That. Nigga." Blow after blow after blow, he attacked her until his arm got tired. He got off of her and kneed her in the rib, cracking it. "Get yo' ass up and get in the back seat. I should have left you in the hood. There's where you wanna go back to, huh?"

Fancii struggled to get up. "No, please." She was out of breath. She forced herself up and into the backseat.

Street Kings 2

She climbed on it and laid out straight. Blood dripped
from her lip. "I'm sorry, Mills. Please, baby. I'm so, so
sorry." She held her ribs and prayed that they weren't
broken. She had to find a way to make him feel better.
She couldn't lose him. He was her ticket into high soci-
ety. She couldn't return to the ghetto, she just couldn't.

Mills pulled out of the gas station. "That nigga say
anything about me, huh?"

Fancii wiped the blood from her mouth. "No, he just
wanted me back. He said..." She hugged herself as a
sharp pain shot through her ribs. "Owww, Mills, you
gotta take me to the hospital. I think you broke my ribs,
baby." She fell back to the floor holding her ribs, taking
short breaths that pained her with every inhale and ex-
hale.

Mills waved her off and got behind the steering
wheel. "You deal wit' that, Fancii. That's your fault.
That should teach you a lesson. From here on out, I
don't want you dealing with Noodles or nobody from
Crenshaw ever again. The next time I find out that you
are, all of the gigs that you've booked on my account
will be stopped, and contracts will be severed. You need
to get it through your head that you are nothing without
me. Noodles can't offer you shit!" he spat, still pissed at
the entire event. He didn't know what type of game that
she and Noodles were playing, but he didn't have time
for it. He'd become addicted to Fancii, and he wanted
her all to himself. He knew that she still had some form
of addiction to Noodles and he wanted to break it so bad.

Fancii climbed to the back seat and winced in terrible pain. Anytime she bent to the right in the slightest, a
mind-numbing pain shot up her right side. Tears ran
down her cheeks. "Please take me to the hospital, baby.

99

I beg of you." She slumped all the way to the floor of the vehicle and curled into a ball.

Mills looked into the rearview mirror and scoffed. "See, that's what you get. Damn. Just hold ya horses I'ma take you to our doctor so you can get the best possible treatment. I love you, Fancii. You need to know that. I love you, and you are mine!"

Chapter 11

Noodles interlocked his fingers as he sat across the oak wood table from Dwayne. They were in Dwayne's mansion's dining room. There was food all over the table: fried chicken, collard greens, pinto beans, white rice, cornbread, German chocolate cake, and ice cream in the freezer. Dwayne wanted to make sure that Noodles was good and stuffed before he left his home. He believed that no matter who you were or where you'd come from, if you were a man, the way to your heart was through your stomach.

Brandi set a plate with all of the fixings in front of Noodles and kissed him on the cheek. "Hope you like everything. Me and my sister been slaving over this stove all day to get things right for you." She rubbed along his shoulder, then walked off with her tight Prada maid uniform clinging to her every curve. The skirt portion was so short that both of her bottom cheeks were exposed. They looked good to Noodles. She was so strapped. With each step she took, her cheeks jiggled. He felt a stirring in his lap.

Kandi came and set a bucket of ice and Moët in the center of the table. She bent all the way over in Noodles's face. Her skirt rose and revealed her pussy lips from the back. Both were shaven, and plump. Her perfume intoxicated his male senses. Without restraint he rested his hand on her ass and squeezed it. She purred and looked back at him. "About time there is some life in you," she teased, and then she walked away from him, swishing hard.

Dwayne sat across the table, amused. Men were so simple, he thought. A little food, keep a bad woman in

101

their face, and blindside them with figures of cash, you could conquer them every time. He was sure of that. He watched Noodles eye the girls until they stepped from the living room and closed the sliding doors, leaving the two men alone.

Noodles grabbed his plate of food and drowned the chicken and collard greens with hot sauce, after cleansing his hands with Purel. He tore into the food, starving. The last couple weeks had been rough for him. They affected his appetite. He'd been down to consuming a meal a day, and now it had finally caught up with him. He bit into the fried chicken breast and ripped the meat from the bone viciously. "So, what's good, Dwayne? Why you call me out here tonight?" he asked, smacking loudly. He grabbed the bottle of champagne and popped the cork. The liquid fizzed over his fingers. He turned the bottle up and downed a third of it.

Dwayne ate with class and meekness. "It seems that I am sliding in the polls. Bronco Banks is getting closer to me. In fact, all that separates us is three points. After his speech yesterday, I'm afraid to even glance at the new numbers." He crushed cornbread over his greens and forked a portion into his mouth.

Noodles was chowing down. He burped and kept right on eating. "So, what that gotta do with me? I been doing everything that you told me to do." His mouth was full of food again.

The sight of his chewed up food and spit took Dwayne's appetite away from him. It was irritating for him to think that Noodles had no home training. He pitied his parents – well, his mother Sondra. He hated Bronco. He dropped his utensils. "Do you remember the proposition I made to you regarding your mother moving from Crenshaw over to the Valley?"

Now Noodles dropped his fork. He finished chewing the chicken in his mouth, smacking loudly. "Yeah, I remember. Why you bringing that shit up? A deal is a deal."

Dwayne nodded his head and pulled at the hairs of his chin. "Yeah, well, it most certainly is. I know I'm willing to hold up my side of things. I mean, I know what your mother means to you, but I don't think your camp does. You see, the problem is not with me; it's with your camp." He cleansed his hands on a wet wipe. He set his briefcase on the table and pulled out a series of photos. He slid them across the table to Noodles.

Noodles sucked his fingers. "I don't know what the fuck you talking about, homie. My camp is in order." He wiped his hands on wet wipes and dried them on a napkin. He picked up the pictures and started to go through them. The sight of Filipino and Bronco Banks sitting at a restaurant talking blew his mind. Then there were another three shots of the two sitting in a drop top Bentley, engrossed in conversation. Others of them walking on a beach laughing. Noodles was confused. "What the fuck is this? What are you showing me?" Picture after picture Noodles flipped through. Each picture seemed to hurt him more than the last.

"Members of your camp are canoodling with the enemy. It has been brought to my attention that Filipino has been working in close proximity with Bronco Banks. He's doing jobs for him. He's murdering, racketeering, raising the crime rate on his behalf. Whenever we do one thing for our cause, he goes out and does two for theirs. In the field, he's what you would call a double agent."

Noodles shook his head in disbelief. His heart was broken. "But this my nigga. He would never do me like that. He know I don't fuck with my old man at all. He know what that fool did to my sister." Noodles was speechless.

"Pictures don't lie, Noodles." Now it was time to pull out the big guns. He presented the manufactured documents. "Did you know that your boy has three hundred thousand dollars tucked away in a Swiss bank account that he is supposed to get upon the election of Bronco Banks? I mean, this is his name right?" Dwayne trailed his finger over Filipino's name and date of birth.

Noodles felt like he'd been gut punched. "What the fuck, Dwayne, why are you showing me this?"

"I'm showing you this so you can know who you're dealing with. Everybody that says they're your friend isn't always your friend. I also have the knowledge that he has gotten your sister, Bronco Banks's daughter Cheyenne, pregnant per the orders of your father in an attempt to bring her back over to his side of the family. Everything is strategic with that man. Everything is strategic, and well-planned by him. I can only imagine what he has in store for you. Only time will tell."

Noodles slammed his fist on the table and stood up. "He ain't got shit planned for me. I'll take his ass out the game before he do anything to me. It ain't sweet over here. Not now, not ever."

Dwayne held up his hands. "Hold the phone, baby. I'm not the enemy. I'm on your side. And before I tell you what I wanna do, I wanna show you something." He pulled out more paperwork. This time it was paperwork that would make Sondra a legal citizen of the United States of America. He slid it across the table. "Upon me being elected, I give you my word that your mother will officially become a legal citizen of the United States of America. On top of that, she will be given a three-story home in the valley with eight bedrooms and four baths, a swimming pool, and two car garage with a truck and a car. Her name will be on all of these things. They will be hers indefinitely. She will officially be able to live out her version of the American dream with no hindrances. In addition to these, you will be given my influence and privilege. I don't know what it is that you look to becoming in the future, but whatever your goals and ambitions are, I will see to it that you are able to obtain them. You have my word on that."

Noodles took a second to take it all in. Dwayne seemed to be offering him a lot. He imagined the look on his mother's face as she stepped foot into her new home and received papers making her a legal citizen. She would no longer have to be on the run from ICE. That alone was priceless. Everything was about her now. He wanted to protect her and give her the best life. She deserved it more than anybody else.

Dwayne smiled at him. He could only imagine what Noodles was mulling over. He'd made the proposition as sweet as possible. No man in their right mind could turn them down. He would get what he wanted. He always did.

Noodles looked into his eyes. "All of this shit sound good, but what do I have to pay you for this? I already know that ain't shit free in this world."

Dwayne smiled, and then his face turned sinister. "I want you to kill Bronco Banks. I don't care how you do it, or where, but I want him out of the game. You take him out of the game, and the red carpet will be rolled out to you. You got my word on that." He stepped around the table and stood before Noodles. "So, tell me, Nadell, what are you going to do?"

***

Filipino sat back on the hospital bed and allowed Cheyenne to sit between his legs and lay her back on his chest. He moved her hair out of the way and kissed her neck. "How you feeling, baby?"

She sighed. "I feel bad about how things went with Noodles. I been thinking about it. Maybe we should have told him about you and me. Then he wouldn't have reacted so crazy. My brother means well. He just has a funny way of showing his emotions."

Filipino took a deep breath and exhaled loudly. Cheyenne's hair blew across her back. He felt remorseful for how things had gone between him and Noodles as well. He loved his homie like a blood brother. They had been through it all together. He never thought that they would fall out over Cheyenne. He had intentions on stopping their rendezvous before Noodles found out. Now that he had found out, things were bound to get crazy. "Cheyenne, do you love me enough to be with me for the rest of your life?"

Cheyenne looked back at him, confused. She frowned her face into a ball. The tape on the bandage popped and attempted to come a loose. "Filipino, what are you talking about?"

He scooted from behind her and stepped on to the hospital floor. "Look, I'm just gon' be honest with you.

You know I like fucking wit' plenty of hoes. I got a weakness for pussy. But if ever I was going to settle down, I would need to know that the woman I'm doing it with wanted me for the rest of her life."

Cheyenne managed to get out of the bed. "Filipino, are you asking me to marry you or something?"

He shrugged his shoulders. "I don't know. Maybe. I mean, I'm the one that got you into this mess, right? Had I not called you the other night when you were set to go out on the town with your mother and Noodles, you would have never been in a shooting and fire and have to be scarred for the rest of your life. This is my fault. So, I have to do the right thing, and the right thing to do is to marry you. You shouldn't have to worry about who's going to accept you because of your injuries when I am the cause of them." Filipino already felt responsible for his mother's death. He had to find a way to reconcile with his conscious. It was killing him.

"So, what you're basically saying is that you want to marry me out of guilt?" Cheyenne was offended.

He shook his head. "No, baby. You're missing what I'm saying. First…listen, I love you. I've always loved you. I had a funny way of showing it because of my need for a plethora of pussy. But now that we've been through this traumatic experience, I see how much you mean to me, and all I wanna be with is you. But in order for me to cross all the way over, I need to know that you love me just as much as I love you. That's all. If you do, then let's do this. Let me put that ring on your finger. So, do you?"

Cheyenne lowered her head. "I don't know what to say, Filipino. Of course, I love you, but with these injuries, my life is going to be so different now. If you love different forms of pussy so much, how do you know that mines will be enough for you? How do you know that you won't see somebody way prettier somewhere and all of your old bad ways won't resurface? How do you know these feelings you're feeling right now won't disappear once the guilt of this situation dies away?"

Filipino ran his hand over his face. "I don't know anything, Cheyenne. I'm nineteen years old. All I know is that I love you right now, in this moment. That I am crazy about you, and that I can see myself being with you for a long time. I need to protect you and keep you safe and sound. I need to love and cherish you. I think that what we've just gone through has allowed me to see things more clearly. I realize how short life is, and how every second that we are given is precious. That's all I know. That's all I see. All I'm asking is that you give me a chance. Please, Cheyenne. Damn." Being emotional was something new for him. He feared her rejecting him, and it started to anger him.

Cheyenne needed more time to think. It was taking her a strange amount of time to process what he was asking and what she was feeling because of it. She didn't like the feeling of being vulnerable. She didn't like to feel dependent on a man. She'd been independent for as long as she could remember. A woman. Strong. Confident in her direction. Now, with her injuries dictating her place in the modeling world - a world of vanity - she honestly felt so confused that she didn't know which way to go with things. "Filipino, I just need some time to think. There are so many thoughts and feelings going through my mind right now that it's crazy. I mean, if we were to take that leap how would we support ourselves? How would we make it?"

Filipino shook his head. "We would. Just know that. I can call in a few favors to get us the things we need. I mean, you're already pregnant with my seed. The logical thing to do would be to marry you, and we figure this shit out together. Damn, all I'm asking is for a shot. That's it."

Cheyenne fell into deep thought for two full minutes. She weighed the pros and cons in her head of being with Filipino. She factored in the pregnancy situation and sighed in defeat. She felt that he deserved a chance. After all, he had saved her life, and she was in love with the young thug.

Filipino walked up to her. "So what do you say, baby? Are we going to do this the right way? Will you give me that chance?" He held her by the waist, peeled the bandage slowly away from her cheek, and kissed the wound there with soft lips.

Cheyenne winced and fluttered in his grasp. Even though she was mildly apprehensive, she heard the words leaving her mouth. "Yeah, baby, let's do this."

"That's all I needed to hear. Now watch me show my ass for you."

Hood Rich

Chapter 12

The helicopter rose from the top of Chase International Building Industries. It ascended into the air. The light from the sun reflected off of its body. Noodles adjusted the headset on his ears and made himself comfortable in his seat. He sipped from a bottle of orange juice. He was high as a kite. His eyes were low. His heart pounded in his chest. All he could think about was his impending mission after accepting Dwayne's offer. Could he really body his own father? He constantly asked himself that question. He carried a severe, utter disdain for the man. He hated him for the way he'd treated their mother, and for his deviant behavior with Cheyenne throughout the years. There had been many nights where he'd laid awake in his bed at night imagining taking Bronco Banks out of the game for his many sins. He never thought he would act on the anger, but now he was not only preparing to do such a thing but being compensated for it. He closed his eyes and allowed for the Percocets to take over his senses. The pills mixed with the Maui Loud had him feeling breezy.

Dwayne sat beside Noodles and looked out of the helicopter's window. It felt good to be mayor. There was no way he would allow for Bronco Banks to take him out of his seat. He hated the man ever since he'd set foot in Los Angeles. First he stole away his precious woman, and then he snatched up every property that his company had set their eyes on first. He felt that Bronco had a serious vendetta against him for no reason at all, and because he did, he had a habit of making nonchalant shots at Dwayne, shots that he picked up on immediately. Now he wanted his mayoral seat. He had dirtied the streets of Los Angeles, used his thugs to take the lives of the people solely for his political gain. Bronco was a sick man. In order to defeat him, Dwayne knew that he must become just as sick. Using his own son to take his life was going to be legendary, the ultimate slap in the face. He couldn't wait until it all fell down. But first, he would give Noodles a taste of the good life. He'd rope him in, get him accustomed to living lavishly. He was sure it would give him more of an incentive to follow through with Bronco Banks's demise. "Say, Noodles, tonight I just want you to enjoy yourself. I don't want you thinking about any of my propositions. I want you to kick back and relax. That's all I ask. Alright?"

Noodles continued to look out at the sun as it began to set. "Like I told you earlier, fuck that nigga." He curled his lip. "Long as you stick to everything you told me that you was going to do, we got a deal."

Dwayne smiled. "My word is golden. That's the first thing you'll come to realize. A man can only be respected by how powerful and true his words are. By words, God spoke everything into existence. Man must learn from that." He sat back in his seat and closed his eyes. "You might wanna catch you a few Z's, Noodles. We'll be arriving at our destination in about two hours. You better revitalize your energy. You'll need it." He clasped his fingers behind his head and yawned.

"Yeah. A'ight." Noodles got comfortable and closed his eyes. Fancii's face came into his mind. He wondered if she was okay. He worried about her, no matter how bad she'd shit on him. She was still the first love of his life. They had history, and his feelings for her would never change. He could tell that she was hooked on something. Her behavior was so unfamiliar. It made her a stranger to him when he'd known her nearly his entire life. He thought about calling her, then thought about how she'd react to his calls, and decided against it. He had to keep her in his past. The future would be promising for him as long as he had Dwayne to pave the way. His first priority had to be securing his mother's stability, then he would focus on himself.

***

Eliza led Filipino through the mansion and down the long corridor that led to Bronco Banks's office. The corridor had soft red carpet with gold trimming. More paintings of famous African American people covered the white walls. Three crystal chandeliers decorated the ceiling before he reached Bronco's door. He stepped up to it and knocked.

Bronco smiled and took his glasses off of his face. He was expecting Filipino. "Come in, son."

Filipino twisted the knob and stepped into the office. It smelled of Somali Rose incense. Bronco stood up and shook his hand. Filipino looked into his eyes and felt like shit. Noodles had told him what Bronco had done to their family, and some of the sexual things he'd done to Cheyenne when she was just a young teenager. He hated the man as strongly as they did, but he needed him. Needed him for seed money. He wanted to do right by Cheyenne, and the only way he would be able to do that is if he used Bronco Banks to get into a financially sound position. Once he locked up a financial deal with him, he would focus on his retaliation towards Combo.

"Please, son, have a seat over here," Bronco encouraged him.

Filipino waved him off. "Look, I ain't got time to be doing a bunch of negotiating and all that shit. I need a large amount of cash, and I need it like a-sap." He was riled up. The China traveled through his system and sped up his brain and thought processes.

Bronco frowned. "What's the matter, son? And what can I do to help you?"

Filipino paced back and forth. Sweat dripped down his neck. "Look man there's two things. The first is that I know who tried to kill me and Cheyenne the other day."

Bronco Banks stood up after sitting in his seat for a split second. "Somebody tried to kill my daughter? Who?" he snapped ready to call in the big guns. "What happened to her?"

Eliza stepped into the office and closed the door behind her. She snuck to the back of the office and sat down. She'd heard the drama from the hallway and wanted to get inside so she could record their conversation. Over the months of working with Bronco, she'd developed a habit of recording everything that took place with the family. She knew it was going to be useful somewhere down the line.

"It's a nigga by the name of Combo. His real name is Antwan. He tried to burn her and myself to death. He's a street goon, been getting it in for a long time. Well known. Cuz got a vendetta against me and Noodles and he trying to take us out of the game. He done already murdered my mother - at least, I believe he did - and now he working on taking us out. You know how that war shit go."

Eliza's eyes got big at the mention of Combo's name. Combo was one of the street toughs that she and Mills had hired to increase the crime rate. She was experiencing a conflict of interest. Unbeknownst to Bronco Banks, he was funding both sides. She shifted uncomfortably on the sofa and continued to use her phone to record the meeting.

"Burn to death? Combo, you say?" He was furious. "Well, do you have an address? If so, give it to me. I'll blow his ass off the face of the earth."

Filipino laughed. His smile turned into a deadly snarl. "Ain nobody gon' kill that clown but me. He took my mother's life and tried to assassinate the mother of my child. Those are two unforgivable sins."

Bronco shook his head. "It sounds like he's been pretty busy. He's gotten away with this shit long enough. Now my daughter is involved. That makes me furious." He slammed his fist on the table so hard that it knocked over his open laptop. His dark face turned darker with a hint of red.

Filipino mugged him. "Bronco, your daughter is the mother of my child. She's pregnant with my seed as we speak. That fool tried to take her life away. I can't let that shit ride, no way, no how."

It was like the wind was released out of Bronco's sails. Pregnant? Cheyenne was pregnant? How could this be? And how could she allow for herself to be impregnated by such a loser? A low life. Scum bag. An idiot with no future other than prison or the grave? "You and Cheyenne? Since when?"

Filipino eyed him from the corners of his eyes. "That ain't important. All you need to know is that she's my heart. I love her, and I want to provide a productive future for her and our child. In order to do that, I'm going to need a nice amount of scratch, so I'm taking all jobs. It looks like you're surging in the polls. A bit more of what we've been doing already oughta send you right over the top. So, what do you got for me?"

Eliza was tapping away on her laptop. She pulled up the addresses of everybody that she knew for sure was a part of Combo's crew. She printed them out and stopped the recording of the office's conversation. "Here, Bronco, these four need to be taken care of like a-sap. They know too much. Have seen too much and are too close to the campaign. It's time that they go, and it'll be a breeze for him because they are from Leimert and Baldwin Village. Areas I know he will know quite well. Here."

Bronco took the sheet from her, looked it over, and handed it to him. "Twenty five grand apiece. The sooner the better. Make sure their bodies drop in Crenshaw. You get paid as soon as the mission is done. There is also one more stipulation."

Filipino took the print out and mugged him. "What's that?"

"I need to see my daughter. I need to sit down and have a conversation with her. I want to be back in her life. It's important to me. Can you talk some sense into her? If you will, I will purchase you guys a house for your impending family." Bronco had no plans of doing any such thing. He wanted to see Cheyenne again so he could talk some sense into her. He couldn't allow for her to bear his seed. It would screw up their bloodline. Filipino's people came from the gutters. They were bums. They had nothing to offer the world. Cheyenne was a Banks. She was supposed to marry a man of class, not of trash. He would find a way to break that up as soon as he could.

Filipino imagined the house. It would be the first steps of the many that would have to be taken. "Bronco, I know how she's going to respond, but I will do my absolute best to persuade her. We need that house."

"You get me two hours with my daughter, and it's yours."

Filipino nodded and looked I've the paperwork. "You got it." He looked over to Eliza. "Any specific order you want me to handle this business?"

She shook her head. "Just as long as they are gone before the week is out. I couldn't care less. Make it good. The more sadistic. the better. We are looking to make a splash on the news. Something like this will help us in the polls dramatically." She stood and extended her hand. "Do we have a deal?"

Filipino looked from her and back over to Bronco and sighed. He shook her hand. "We have a deal. I'ma get on this immediately."

Hood Rich

Chapter 13

Brandi sashayed across the white carpet in her bare feet. Her pretty French-tipped toes dug into the carpet. She wore a white one piece Victoria's Secret bikini. The bottom cuffed her mound so tightly that her sex lips were visible. She carried a bottle of Patron in her hand. She took a seat on Noodles's lap. She placed one ankle over each of his thighs, opening her legs wide. Once there, she sucked on his neck, moaning. "Are you ready for this?"

Kandi knelt beside them in a red one piece Victoria's Secret bathing suit. She kissed along Noodles's thigh. She opened his legs and pulled his piece out of his boxers. She stroked it and ran her thumb over the apple head. Her tongue lashed out at it. She twirled it round and round before sucking him into her mouth swallowing him as far as she could. She gagged and pulled her head off of him. Then she was sucking swiftly.

Noodles moaned in the penthouse suite. He rubbed Brandi's front. He squeezed her pussy lips together over and over. Her kitten was chubby. He moved the material to the side and exposed her shaved pussy. He ran his finger up and down it. She was already drooling between her folds. He sucked the finger into his mouth.

"Damn, you got a big dick," Kandi said out loud. She couldn't believe how heavy he felt in her hand. She couldn't wait to sit on it. She licked along its length, sucked him back into her mouth, and watched as he fingered Brandi. Her digits snuck between her own legs and entered into her slippery garden of love. The scene was driving her crazy. She sucked faster and faster.

Brandi humped forward into his fingers. She sucked on his neck and scraped it with her teeth. "Don't you wanna fuck me, Noodles? Huh. Can't you see how wet my pussy is for you?" she asked with her eyes closed.

Noodles felt Kandi sucking him hard. It felt so good. He groaned and tried to catch his breath. His hips humped forward. "Hell yeah. Hell yeah. I want both sisters. Both of y'all finna give me some of that pussy." He pushed Brandi off of his lap, stood up, and pulled his boxers down. His big dick bobbed in the air. He rolled a condom over it and stroked the monster. He sat on the edge of the bed and scooted all the way back.

Brandi was the first to make it to him. She took ahold of his dick and sucked it into her mouth. She slurped up and down it and then offered it to Kandi. "Huh, girl, let's drive his ass crazy."

Kandi held his dick along with Brandi. She sucked up and down it, looking into his eyes. It felt so good in her mouth. Hot and thick. The head was spongy. It throbbed and telescoped like a light saber. This delighted her. She loved to have control over men, loved to have them at her mercy, and whenever she put her mouth on their pieces, she took them on a journey that she orchestrated. She felt powerful.

Brandi pulled the piece out of Kandi's hands and sucked him hard and fast. Her fingers played inside of her pussy. She anticipated the fucking that was sure to come. She wanted him bad. Wanted him ever since she'd laid her eyes upon him. There was something about his dark skin and rough exterior that drove her crazy. Noodles grabbed Brandi by the hair and brought her to his face. He kissed all over her lips. He reached between her thighs and rubbed her cat. This made Kandi suck him harder and faster.

"Let's turn up, shawty. Mmm. Let's turn up. Get yo' thick ass up here."

Brandi straddled him. She pulled his piece out of Kandi's mouth and slowly slid back on it with her eyes closed. "Uhhhhhhhh. Yes," she moaned.

Kandi came around and kissed Noodles's lips. Her tongue lashed out at him. She rubbed his stomach and squeezed his chest. "How that feel, Brandi? Is it opening you up?" Kandi wanted to know while Noodles fingered her.

Brandi held his shoulders and bounced up and down on his dick. The springs of the bed squeaked. She pulled down the arm straps of her bathing suit and exposed her caramel breasts. They hopped up and down. "Uh. Uh. Uh. It's good. Oooh. Shit. It's good. Kandi. Just. Wait." She looked between her thighs and saw their connection. The way his piece stretched her to capacity. It drove her crazy.

Kandi kicked around his navel. She sucked along his thighs, then laid on her side beside him with her thighs open. She ran a finger along her slit. "Taste me Noodles. Please." She opened her lips and exposed her strawberry-colored center.

Noodles grabbed her by the ass and pulled her closer to his face. Once there, his tongue invaded her sex lips. He traveled up and down her crease, trailed circles around her pleasure bud. Sucked it into his mouth.

"Uhhhhhhhh!" Kandi screamed. She began to hump into his face at full speed while he held her ass cheeks.

The sight drove Brandi mad. She pulled on her own nipples and rode him faster. He went deep inside of her.

With every stroke she opened her mouth and tilted her head backward. She gasped for breath. The pleasure was in insurmountable. His width alone was enough to bring on her first orgasm. "Noodles. Noodles. Aw shit. I'm cumming. I'm cumming!" She bounced higher and higher, squeezing his dick with her velvety walls.

Noodles could feel her gripping him. Her juices poured into his center. The feeling was familiar. It ignited the animal inside of him. He held her hips and slammed her down on to him over and over while she came in a fury of shouts and spasms. His tongue continued to twirl around and around Kandi's clitoris.

Brandi came hard and collapsed on top of him. Her breathing was ragged. Her kitty vibrated on the inside. She felt Kandi push her off of him. She wound up in her back with her thighs wide open, playing in between her lips.

Her clit was rock hard. She pulled the lips back and looked it over before pinching it and sending chills up and down her spine.

Kandi straddled Noodles in the reverse cowgirl. She pulled his condom off and sucked his dick into her mouth. She ran up and down the length of it for a full minute, then rolled a new rubber over it before inserting his penis into her. She opened her thighs wide and popped forward, engulfing him. "Unh. Watch my ass, Noodles. Watch it, and smack when you feel like it." She humped forward and cocked back. Humped forward, and twisted her hips, riding him fast, her fat booty jiggling with every stroke.

Brandi sucked on Noodles's neck while he rubbed all over Kandi's booty and groaned deep within her throat. Kandi's pussy was just a bit tighter and slightly wetter. He could feel her walls clenching and unclenching his pole while she rode him. Her ass cheeks were opened wide enough for him to see a peek of her crinkle back there. He smacked that fat ass hard and watched it jiggle.

"Uh! Shit. Baby! Smack it! Aww, fuck!" she moaned, and then sped up the pace. She held on to his ankles for leverage and went berserk on his dick.

Noodles fingered Brandi and tongued her down. She held her pussy lips open for him. His eyes rolled into the back of his head. Kandi was doing a number on him. "Ride me, shawty. Ride me. Shit. Shit. Shit." he groaned, feeling his seed rise in his balls.

Brandi sucked his nipples and nipped at them with her teeth. Her hand rubbed his stomach and played around with his pubic hairs. She rested her fingers on the bottom of his greasy pole. Felt him fingering her faster and faster.

Kandi went berserk. She was riding him so fast that it sounded like a bunch of people were jumping in the bed. "Uh! Uh! I'm cumming, baby. I'm cumming. Shit. Smack my ass. Smack my ass. Smack it hard, shit!"

Noodles pulled his wet fingers out of Brandi and smacked her ass hard over and over. He smacked and squeezed that big booty. "Cum, bitch. Cum on this dick. Aww, fuck, I'm cumming too."

Kandi felt his dick jerking like crazy. That sent her off. Her orgasm rocked her body. She rode him as fast as she could and screamed. "Fuck, Noodles! Fuck me!" She got to shaking and riding him with quick spasms before falling in between his legs. His dick popped out of her, greasy and hard. The head of it was sticking through the rubber. It was shooting like a geyser.

Brandi grabbed it and sucked it into her mouth. She sucked hard with her eyes closed. milking him of his manly essence. She got globs at a time and swallowed, loving the taste of him. She popped him out. "Mmm, Noodles." She stroked his piece. "I knew you was a beast." She smiled and looked up at him, then sucked him back into her mouth and went to work.

Noodles rubbed all over her fluffy ass cheeks. He slid his fingers into her slit. He still couldn't believe how meaty the both of them were. "Y'all got some good pussy. I gotta give the both of you that," he admitted.

Kandi kissed his lips. "Well, it seem like you gon' be around for a long time. I hope you plan on enjoying us again and again." She licked his lips. She could taste the pussy upon them.

Dwayne stepped into the room, smoking a Cuban cigar. He smiled and sniffed the air. "Smell like y'all been having fun in here."

Kandi pulled Noodles's piece away from Brandi and sucked it into her mouth again. Her head worked up and down it while she looked Dwayne in the eyes. She knew the man put up a front. Anytime he saw the sisters enjoying someone, he was more apt to ending their communication with the person. She wanted to enjoy the rod in her hand before it was taken away from them for good.

"Well, Noodles, now that you've had your recess, I think it's time that we get down to business. What do you say?"

Noodles slid his fingers into Brandi. "Tomorrow is a new day. I still got a lot of hard dick to give out." He pulled Kandi down and got between her thighs. "You got a problem wit' that Dwayne?"

The mayor puffed his cigar and laughed. "Nall, son, do ya thang. You're right; tomorrow is another day."

***

Filipino slid through the back bathroom window and fell into the bathtub. He remained still for thirty seconds, before getting up and looking around. He stepped out of the tub and pulled his Forty Glock from his waistband. He screwed the silencer in place and came to the bathroom door, listening with his ear pressed against it. It was three o'clock in the morning, and he was getting ready to knock off the first person upon his list. Bronco promised him twenty five thousand apiece for each person he knocked off, and he looked forward to every penny of the money. He had to get himself together to insure that he could provide a productive life for Cheyenne and the child that she was carrying. He was tired of being a failure. He felt it was time to grow up and get his shit together. The loss of his mother, and the two near death experiences for himself, had been eye-opening.

He twisted the knob of the bathroom and slowly pulled it open. It creaked at first. He cringed and stayed in place. He waited for a few seconds, and then pulled it open some more. He stuck his head out of it and saw that he was in the enemy's kitchen. There was a night light over the sink. Roaches crawled all over the walls. It smelled like the garbage needed to be taken out. The heat seemed to be cranked up so high that Filipino felt himself sweating under his arms already. He scratched at the ski mask and held the gun shoulder high. He stepped out of the bathroom and into the kitchen. Stood

125

still. There was the sound of music playing. Ella Mai. He smiled under the mask and sniffed the air again. Sure enough, there was the scent of sex in the air. The mark must have been getting it in, he thought.

The kitchen was attached to a back bedroom. The door was closed. He stepped next to it and listened. He heard the sounds of moaning and groaning. He nodded and stepped away from it. The next five minutes would be spent searching all over the house to ensure that no one else was present. After confirming that to be the case, he was back standing in front of the back room door. His heart beat fast in his chest. He grabbed ahold of the knob and slowly twisted it.

The door slowly opened. The scent of fornication, and the sounds of Ella Mai's "Weekend", grew louder. There was the squeaking of the bed. Moans and grunts. Filipino frowned. He pushed the door all the way open and aimed toward the pair on the bed before finger fucking his trigger.

Boof. Boof. Boof. Boof. Boof.

The pair never had a chance. He watched them fall all over each other. The white sheets turned a bright shade of red, and then they were unmoving, both the male target and his female counterpart. Filipino turned the stove on so the gas would travel through the house, then peeked inside of the room again. They were laced. He slowly closed the door and exited the house the same way he had come.

One down, three to go.

Chapter 14

Noodles stepped inside of the hospital room and took a deep breath. He slowly made his way over to Cheyenne's bedside. It felt good to see her sitting up. He stepped in front of her and rubbed her cheek. "Hey, Goddess. How they treating you in here?" he asked, sort of nervous. He prayed that they could communicate cordially. He was worried about his sister. The sun shone through the big window inside Cheyenne's room. It was ninety plus degrees outside, hot and humid.

Cheyenne shrugged her shoulders. "Okay, I guess. They're letting me check out of here today. They gave me my last skin graft yesterday and monitored my lungs overnight. It seems that everything is getting back to normal. Physically, I feel a bit drained, but I am ready to get out of here." She fluffed her pillow. "What brings you here?"

Noodles walked to the window and looked out of it before turning his back to her. Four robins flew past the window before disappearing over the building. "I found out you were checking out today, and before you did, I just wanted to have a sibling conversation with you. I mean, if that wouldn't be a problem." He turned around to face her.

Cheyenne lowered her eyes and tried to calm herself down. She never liked when Noodles - or anybody, for that matter - spoke to her in innuendos. She was a straightforward person, and that's how she wished to communicate. "Noodles, why don't you just tell me what's on your mind so we can get an understanding? You know I don't like when you beat around the bush."

"A'ight, but before I do, I just need to know that I can trust you, and that whatever I say to you will stay in this room. Will it, Sis? I mean, you can't even let Filipino know because it's that serious."

Before the words rolled off of his tongue, Filipino sauntered into the room with a bag of barbecue. He wanted to give Cheyenne a welcome home meal before she even left the hospital. "Can't let me know what?" he asked, mugging Noodles.

Noodles clenched his jaw. "Damn, homie, don't you know how to knock?"

Filipino set the two bags of food on Cheyenne's table. "Tell me what?" He looked from Cheyenne to Noodles then back to Cheyenne again.

"I don't know, baby. He just got here a few minutes before you did. But I need you to step out of the room so I can holler at my brother. Clearly there is something on his mind, and I, for one, wanna know what it is."

Filipino mugged Noodles and stepped across the room toward him. "I think it's time me and you get an understanding too, homie. Ain't no sense in us walking around with a bunch of animosity. You know we handle shit. Like men." Filipino cracked his knuckles and curled his upper lip.

Noodles stepped into his grill. "Soon as I'm done here, we can handle that bidness. You ain't said nothing but a word. But for now, let me holler at my sister in private. This family bidness." He shot daggers into his eyes.

"Damn, why y'all gotta beef over nothing? Both of our families are under attack, and all you two idiots wanna do is go at each other's throats. What for?" Cheyenne asked.

Filipino pointed at Noodles. "This nigga got a problem wit' me because I'm fucking wit' you. He on some sucka shit, and it's time he get over it."

"Nigga, you don't tell me what to get over. That's my ma'fuckin' sister right there. Her and my mother been all I had until I met yo' stupid ass. I don't give a fuck what y'all got going on, she still my heart. You should have told me what it was, and since you didn't, we gotta knuckle up. It's gon' be tension until we do so," Noodles assured him.

"Shid, nigga, close the door. We can handle this bidness right here. We already in a hospital. You know how I get down." Filipino got ready to pull his shirt over his head.

"No! Stop it. Stop it right now. If y'all wanna do that shit, that's cool, but you ain't gon' do it here, and you ain't gon' do it in front of me. Filipino, you leave. Let me holler at him for fifteen minutes, then me and you can decide what we're going to do, baby. I love you. Now go."

Filipino mugged Noodles with hatred. He was fresh off of a kill, so that part of his psyche was screwed up. His long-term homie reminded him of an enemy that needed to be slain. He nodded his head. "Yeah, a'ight. I'ma step off for the moment. I love you too though, Cheyenne. I'll be back in fifteen minutes. Y'all do what you gotta do until then." He left the room and slammed the door behind him.

Noodles stood with his head down. His heart beat fast in his chest. He clenched and unclenched his fists. He was trying his best to calm down, but it was so hard. Filipino had him heated, and their "love you" exchanges only added fuel to the fire. He didn't think that Filipino truly loved his sister. He knew how much his right-hand man loved a variety of pussy. He knew that it was only a matter of time before Filipino hurt Cheyenne. Every time he imagined it, the vision nearly drove him crazy.

Cheyenne looked him over with much-needed patience. "Noodles, you need to let that go and come over here and tell me what's good." She sat on the side of the bed. "Come on, with yo' jealous ass."

He smirked. "Shut up. It ain't about me just being jealous. This shit is just new for me, that's all. I know how me, and the homie get down – well, how I used to get down before I really became serious about Fancii - and I can't honor that nigga fuckin' wit' you. You love too hard, and now with the new physical developments since this fire, I just ain't tying to imagine you being at no dude's mercy. I'd rather smoke bruh before I let that happen. You still my sister. I ain't going."

"Boy, you act like I can't take care of myself. You ain't like I'm so fuckin' naive that I'm just going to let a man run all over me. Noodles, scars or not, I am still a Queen. These injuries and burn marks don't, and can't, define who I am as a woman. Filipino ain't going to do nothing to me that I am against. And besides all of that, just because I'm dealing with him doesn't mean that you aren't my brother. Our bond is still first and foremost. But Noodles, you have to understand that I am having his baby now. We are going to have some form of a relationship, whether you are with or against it. There can't be a fight every time you two come into the same room. That'll get old real fast."

Noodles shrugged his shoulders. "Yeah, I guess. But anyway, I don't wanna talk about that shit right now. Me and him gon' get it up with these knuckles, but until then, we have more pressing issues to worry about. I need you to hear me out." He took a deep breath and began to pace back and forth.

Cheyenne situated herself on the bed and gave him her undivided attention. "I'm ready to listen when you're ready to speak."

"I don't know how to say this shit so I'm just gon' come right out and say it. I gotta take care of our father. I been given one hell of an opportunity, one that I need to take for the betterment of our futures, and I'm finna take it. But before I do, I just wanted to run things by you first."

"What do you do mean take care of him? You planning on being his slave or something, or maybe one of his butlers?" She was confused.

"Nall, what I mean is that I'm finna body his ass for the right amount of cash and opportunity. I been wanting to do it ever since he did that bullshit to you, but I kept my composure because of moms. I respected her by allowing him to keep breath in his body longer then I should have. It's over wit' for that shit."

Cheyenne swallowed. "Are you serious?"

"Very. Pops ain't been nothing but a problem for all of us ever since we came to Los Angeles. It's been one pain after the next. Dude don't give a fuck about our family. We been struggling in Crenshaw while he lives in the suburbs since forever. Now it's time to use his ass for the advancement of our family. That's the way shit gotta go. What are you thinking?"

Cheyenne lowered her head and tried her best to clear her mind. Murder? Their father? As much as she disliked the man for the things he'd done to her, she still couldn't fathom one of them killing him. He was still their father. It was biblically wrong, if nothing else. "Noodles, if you want my honest to God opinion, I just don't think you should do it. I mean, he is still our father, no matter how many transgressions he's waged against us. It's not right."

"Bodying somebody will never be right, Cheyenne. Damn. But it's the game that I am a part of. It is what it is. Like I said before, I just wanted to hear what you thought. You told me, and I'll take it into consideration." Noodles was wishing that he'd never said anything to her now. He wished he would have kept his big mouth shut. The act of getting rid of Bronco Banks was going to be difficult.

Cheyenne climbed out of the bed and walked up to him. "Noodles, what's going on in your brain? You think by taking our father out that it's going to make things better for us? Are you sure you're ready to live with that type of guilt?"

"I gotta do what I gotta do for our family because if I don't, then we'll never have anything. Don't nobody give a fuck about us. Not about you. Not Mama, not me. Her house been shot up five times now over the years. Now it's officially gone. You're lying in a fuckin' hospital bed while Bronco's stepdaughter lays her head on a pillow in Bel-Air. They live in a gated community while we dodge bullets on a regular basis and pray that we'll live to make it through the day. You think it's fair? You honestly thinks that man cares about us?"

"It's not about him caring about us. It's about you taking his life for a price. In addition to that, we can't allow for what he did to us, or how he left us, dictate our futures. We are still in control of our own destinies. No man can take that away from us. Only you, and I can relinquish that power, and I'm not giving mine away. Not to him, not to nobody. Not now, not ever. If killing him is what you want to do, then go right ahead. I swear I won't lose one wink of sleep. Life will go on. But I will let you know this: I will be very disappointed in you. You are better than that."

"Damn, Cheyenne." He balled up his face. "I just shouldn't have said shit to yo' ass. I should have known you were going to send me on some kind of a guilt trip. Now you got my head all screwed up."

"It's because you know I'm right. You know you can't cause any harm to our father. It doesn't matter how trifling he is, or how many nights I had to suffer through his abuse. We have to leave his punishment in God's hands. The battle is not ours."

Noodles stared at her, lost. He shook his head and scoffed. "After all he did to us, you can still have mercy on his punk ass? You something else, you know that?"

She laughed. "I know. But we gon' be alright though. God gon' make a way." She slid her arms around his waist and laid her head on his chest. "Noodles, I don't have all of the answers. All I know is that I love you, and I don't want to see you out here making stupid, impulsive decisions. You're a better man than that. Your job isn't to take care of me and Mama. It's to take care of yourself first and foremost. Once you take yourself out of the trenches, then you can come back and lift us up. The progress has to start somewhere."

Noodles hugged her and released her. "Look, Cheyenne, I don't know what I'm going to do yet. I got a lot of thinking to do. Right now, our old man is the key to a hell of a safe. All I gotta do is cash his ass in, and it'll be rightfully so too. I'ma chill for now. Think shit over more thoroughly. I heard you out, and that's just that." He smiled weakly at her. "You got some money in your pocket?"

She pursed her lips at him. "Why, you gon' give me some?"

He laughed and pulled out a five thousand dollar knot. "You already know I got you. Huh, this five bands. I don't know what you and bruh finna do, but whenever you need anything until you get on your feet, you make sure you hit my phone. I'm always gon' be on the other end for you. I'm always gon' have your back." He pulled her to him and hugged her tight.

Cheyenne smiled. "One thing I can say about you, Noodles, is that you've always been a great brother. I really do love you. And you mean he world to me. Even though I won't want you doing anything as crazy as that, I know that you're your own man, and I'm letting you know right now that I wouldn't love you any less. Just be smart, and careful. Oh, and give me my money." She stepped back and snatched it from him.

Noodles busted up laughing. He missed his sister. Every time he looked at her, he wanted to protect her and do the most for her. She was his heart. "Where you and bruh supposed to be staying?"

"Right now, it's in a hotel outside of Baldwin Village. We'll be there for a few weeks, and then we're going to move into a place on the east side."

Filipino knocked on the door and twisted the knob and stepped in. "Time's up. I hope y'all talked about everything y'all needed to, 'cause from here on out, me and her ain't keeping secrets from one another." He stepped in front of Cheyenne, knelt down on one knee, then pulled the box that contained the three carat diamond ring out of his pocket.

Cheyenne felt her heart skip a beat. She suddenly became breathless. She covered her mouth with her right hand. "What are you doing, Filipino?"

He took a hold of her left hand. "Cheyenne, I love you, ma. I have always been crazy about you, but now I'm ready as a man to take things to the next level. I am asking you to marry me. Give me the opportunity to show you that I am supposed to be your husband despite my flaws. Marry me, baby."

She blinked, and a lone tear sailed down her cheek. "Baby, I don't know what to say. I mean, I love you too." ..."

Noodles stood frozen. He wanted to break it up so bad that it was killing him. Instead he remained in place, clenching his jaw off and on.

Filipino opened the box. The light from the sun shone on the diamond and made it twinkle in the sun rays. "Cheyenne Banks, will you be my wife?"

She smiled and jumped into the air. "Yes, baby. Yes. I'll be your wife."

Filipino slid the ring on to her finger and stood up. He hugged her and twirled her around in the hospital room while Noodles exited with intense anger. Filipino didn't give a fuck. It was all about Cheyenne. His rib. And soon to be his wife.

Hood Rich

Chapter 15

"Now to your left, darling. Give me one of those million dollar smirks. Perfect. Again. Oh my God, she's a natural. These photos are going to be glorious for our swimsuit collection. You're a star," the photographer said as he directed Fancii into different poses.

Mills stood back and watched as Fancii seem to float through the Covergirl set. The other models that were around him whispered about Fancii. They hated how beautiful she was, how she was both slim and curvy in all the right places. He watched the reaction from the men on set and saw how they couldn't take their eyes off of her. This made him both jealous and furious. He hated when other men gawked at his woman. He felt that he owned her. That he had made her. That she belonged to solely him.

Fancii finished her shoot. She slid a robe onto her shoulders without bothering to close it and jogged off set. She came over and slid her arms around his neck. "Baby, did you hear him? I'm doing so good," she mused, proud of herself.

Mills slightly pushed her off of him and took ahold of her wrist. He led her to the hallway where the bathrooms were. Once there, he slammed her against the wall. "Fancii look at your robe. What I tell you about when you leave the set? Huh?"

Fancii was confused. "Baby, what did I do wrong? I just left the set."

A tall blond model came out of the bathroom and looked them over. She smiled weakly and continued on her path.

Mills grabbed her hand, pulled her into the bathroom, and locked the door. He smacked her across the face, dropping her to the floor. He locked the bathroom door and pursued her.

Fancii scooted backwards. "Mills. Please. What did I do? What did I do?"

He pulled her up and placed his nose against hers. "Who do you belong to, Fancii? Tell me, I wanna hear it."

"You-u-u," she stuttered. "I belong to you, Mills. I'm your property."

Mills felt a surge of adrenalin travel through him. He hiked up Fancii's robe and lifted her up on the bathroom sink. He dropped his pants and entered her.

"Uhhh," she moaned, throwing her head back. "Mills, wait."

But it was of no use. Mills plunged in and out of her at full speed. He replayed the scene from just a few minutes prior. How it seemed that everyone was all over Fancii, giving her compliment after compliment. It drove him crazy and made him incredibly jealous at the same time. "You belong to me, Fancii. You. Belong. To. Me." Faster and faster he screwed her.

Fancii dug her nails into his shoulder blades and sucked her bottom lip to keep from screaming out loud. Mills was a pure savage as he took her. He grunted and groaned his way to an orgasm, before leaving her tunnel full of his juices. After he finished he pulled out and forced Fancii to her knees. She took him orally while he wrapped his fingers into her hair. "Fancii, I'm the reason you living this life. Ain't I? You're here because of me. Right?"

Fancii continued to suck him. She nodded her head, popped him out of her mouth, and stroked him. "Yes, Mills, and I appreciate you, baby. I appreciate you with everything that I am."

He tightened his fingers in her hair and slammed back into her mouth. The power made him feel like a giant. He still couldn't quite put his finger on why he had to control her, but the power drove him insane. The more he controlled Fancii, the further he fell in love with her, and he didn't want anybody else even looking at her. He was becoming sick, and the feeling was getting worse by the day. "When you done, baby…aw, fuck." He watched her sucking him, and it gave him chills. "I'm taking you shopping on Rodeo Drive. Anything you want. Fuck, it's so good, baby. Anything you want," he moaned.

Fancii didn't know how to feel. Her only thought was that it might be time to break away from Mills. He was becoming too controlling, possessive, and abusive. While the good life was a fun life to live, the injuries on a day-to-day basis were becoming too much. She found herself being torn down mentally and physically. Emotionally she felt diseased and incredibly damaged. But all it took was one thought of going back to life back in Crenshaw, and it caused her to straighten up. While she was making headway in the modeling industry, she was sure that the clear path was only because of her affiliation with the Banks family. All of the girls in the industry were so beautiful. The competition amongst women was crazy. She was sure that without the Banks family, there would be no modeling gigs. *I'ma ride Mills until I get to where I need to be, then I'ma drop his ass and live my best life. I'ma seize every opportunity that I can while we're together, and then when I climb as high as I can, he's history,* she thought. A sudden smile came across her face as she continued to perform her duties for him.

There was a knock on the door by the client. "Fancii, come on, darling, we're ready for round two. These are the pictures that are going to place you on billboards all over Paris. Chop, chop, Sugar," he ordered clapping his hands together.

"I'll be right there," she promised, standing up.

Mills stepped into her face and brushed her hair back. He grabbed her by the neck and tongued her down. He gripped her backside. The kiss lasted for thirty seconds. "I love you, baby. Now go out there and knock 'em dead."

Fancii looked into his eyes and felt nothing but hatred and anger. She smiled and hugged him. "Thank you, baby. Everything I do is for you. You're my muse," she lied. *Yeah, as soon as I'm big enough, his ass is out of here. I miss Noodles so much.* She wanted to break down into tears.

Another knock on the door and she was out of the bathroom and back to work, feeling lower than scum.

***

Noodles stepped in the middle of the railroad tracks and held his arms out. The bright lights that lined the tracks of Crenshaw illuminated him just enough. He'd taken his shirt off and thrown it to the ground in a fit of anger and frustration. "Nigga, you already know what this is," he shouted to Filipino.

Filipino pulled his shirt over his head and dropped it to the rocks that were on the side of the tracks. He unsnapped the bulletproof vest and dropped it on top of his shirt. "Bruh, you ain't saying shit. You wanna get it in, then let's handle this bidness." He stepped in the middle of the tracks and put up his guards. "Come on."

Noodles mugged him for a minute. He thought about all of the ways that Filipino had betrayed him, and he felt murderous. He was praying that when it came time to them getting down that he could pull back before he hurt him severely. He knew he had a bad temper. It was his Achilles heel. "A'ight then."

The full moon shone high in the sky. The mosquitoes were out in full force. A short distance away they could hear the highway as cars traveled back and forth. Even though it was night, it felt like it was a hundred plus degrees. Los Angeles was experiencing one of the hottest summers on record.

"Well, ain't no sense in standing around. Let's get this show on the road," Filipino said. He rushed Noodles, swinging big, heavy blows.

Noodles blocked one, but got caught by the second and third one, one to the jaws and another to the side of the head. His foot got caught in one of the tracks. He slipped and went down to one knee. The blows that he'd received throbbed painfully.

Filipino saw him go down and jumped back. Had it been anybody else he would have rushed and finished them. But this was Noodles. His partner in crime. His right-hand man, and soon to be brother-in-law. "Get up, Noodles. Come on."

Noodles wiggled his Jordan shoe out of the track and wiped his face with his gloved hands. He glared at

Filipino and jumped up. "Nigga, don't take no pity on me. Next time I fall down, you finish me. That's how this shit go!"

Filipino waved him off. "Whatever, nigga. Get yo' ass up and get some more of these." He tightened his guards and prepared for Noodles to come at him hard.

Noodles moved forward, and when he got into striking distance, he faked as if he was going to swing with his left, ducked, and came with a right hook, rattling Filipino. Before Filipino could fall back Noodles rushed him, picked him up into the air, and dumped him on his back as hard as he could.

Filipino bounced off of the rocks and wound up on his side. He groaned in pain and struggled to get up. The wind had been knocked out of him momentarily. He wheezed. Little rocks were stuck to his back. He crawled on his knees with blood dripping from his mouth.

Noodles kicked him in the ass. "Let's go, fool. You man enough to fuck my sister behind my back. Get her pregnant. Nigga, you man enough to take this ass whoopin'." He kicked him again.

Filipino caught his breath and came to his feet. He spit blood on to the tracks. "I love Cheyenne. I'ma take care of her, and our child. I'ma get myself together and leave this street shit alone, Noodles. I ain't mean to betray you. Shit just happened." He rushed Noodles, swinging.

Noodles tried to back up and stumbled. He braced himself, and ran forward, swinging just as wild and hard as Filipino. Their blows connected with each other's faces and necks. Then they were wrestling, falling to the rocks, grunting and groaning. Noodles wound up on top.

He grabbed Filipino by the neck and dug his nails into him. "That's my only sister, nigga, and if you hurt her, I swear to God I'll kill you. If you don't take care of y'all baby, I'ma kill you again. Nigga, you hear me!" he snapped.

Filipino humped upward and tried to toss him off of his body. He wiggled from his grasp and jumped up breathing hard. Before Noodles could get back up, he rushed him again. He punched Noodles in the jaw and tackled him back to the ground.

Noodles was dizzy, his strength dying out of him. The blow to his jaw affected him greatly. He tried the best he could to put up a fight, but he was in La-La-land. The world seemed to be spinning. The moon looked underfoot.

Filipino straddled him and held him down. "Now you listen to me. I don't need you telling me how to do right by Cheyenne. That's my woman, and that's my child that she's carrying. I got her, and I got our baby. Period."

Noodles struggled against him. His equilibrium was thrown off. "Let me up, Filipino. Let me up right now." He pushed him as hard as he could and jumped up, staggered around on his feet. "Nigga, you bogus. You know you bogus," he spat.

Filipino stood up. About four hundred yards away, he made out the train on its tracks. "Bruh, I told you I apologize. I ain't mean to go behind yo' back, but I did. I can't change that. All I can do is make sure that I take care of her and do right by her. As a man, you gotta let me step up to my responsibilities. I don't fail."

The train screeched along the tracks loudly. It was close enough to cast its lights upon them.

"You damn right you gon' do right by my sister, Filipino. If you don't..." Noodles took off running in his direction.

Filipino braced himself for the impact. Noodles tackled him onto the tracks, and head-butted him in the face, busting his nose. Then he was on top of him, raining blow after blow. He imagined Filipino laughing behind his back as he fucked Cheyenne. It infuriated him. He plowed him with more blows, no longer in his right mind. He stood up and saw that he'd knocked Filipino clean out. His right-hand man was unmoving. Noodles glanced down the tracks and saw the train coming. He stood back and jumped off of the tracks. "I should let you die, nigga. That way you can't be around to hurt my sister!" he hollered.

The train blew its horn and kept chugging along on the tracks. Its horn sounded louder and louder. The ground rumbled. More horn blowing. Filipino remained still, slumped in the middle of the tracks.

Noodles watched him. He looked to his right and saw the train approaching.

It seemed to be coming slowly but making up the distance at a fast pace. He thought about letting him stay on the tracks. Thought about letting the train take him out of the game. He'd betrayed him. Not only was he sleeping with his sister behind his back, but he was working with his father. Both sins were unforgivable. In the moment, he hated Filipino.

The rumbling of the tracks woke Filipino out of his slumber. His eyes bucked wide open. His heart beat fast. He sat up and came to his knees. The train closed in. Chugging. Chucking on the tracks. It blew its horn for the fourth time. Filipino, in a last ditch effort, jumped up and hopped off of the tracks just as the train flew past, blowing their clothes.

Noodles stood with his face turned into a scowl. He felt remorseless. He wished the train had taken Filipino out of the game. If it had, the burden wouldn't have been placed on him to do so.

Filipino fell to his back as the train flew past. His chest heaving up and down. The lines had been drawn in the sand. He now without a shadow of a doubt knew where he and Noodles stood, and as much as it hurt him to know that their bond had been severed, he appreciated being in the know. He jumped up and took off running while the train rumbled past on the tracks separating him and Noodles.

Hood Rich

Chapter 16

Filipino stumbled into the hotel room and fell on the floor. He was shirtless. Blood dripped from his lips. His ribs felt like they were broken. He struggled to catch his breath.

Cheyenne hopped up. "Baby, what happened to you?" She rushed to his side and knelt beside him.

Filipino grabbed a handful of the blanket and pulled himself up. "That nigga almost let me die, Cheyenne. I almost got hit by a muthafuckin' train fuckin' wit' him!" he hollered.

Cheyenne sat beside him. "Who, baby? Who are you talking about?"

"Noodles!" he snapped, and then stood up. He held his ribs and staggered into the bathroom.

"What is going on with you two now? I thought all of that stuff was squashed." She followed him into the bathroom and stood behind him as he ran the water.

Filipino washed his face. He spit blood into the sink. "Cheyenne, I love you, but I think I might have to handle my bidness wit' Noodles. That nigga was finna let that train kill me. Had I not jumped off of those tracks when I did, I would have been dead right now. I don't know what his problem is, but he off of his rocker. Ain't no telling what that nigga finna do next. But I'll tell you what, I ain't finna wait around to find out. If he want beef, then I'ma give his ass a whole cow." He stumbled out of the bathroom and searched through his suitcase until he found a new bullet proof vest. He pulled two plastic Glocks from under the bed and cocked them one at a time.

Cheyenne's eyes were big. "What are you finna do with them?" She pulled his shoulder and turned him around so he could face her.

"I already told you what I'm finna do. That nigga crazy. He probably out there right now mounting up so he can come and take me out. I know how your brother is. I been jamming wit' that nigga since the beginning of this whole murder thing. When he off his rocker like this, ain't no reasoning with him."

"So, you think you just about to go out and kill him? What type of shit is that?" Cheyenne was beside herself with rage. "Y'all need to figure this shit out the right way without use of guns and weapons. Damn. Y'all been friends your whole lives, and you're telling me you can't let this go?"

All of the words she were saying were going into one of Filipino's ears and out of the other. He already felt he knew what he had to do. He had to get Noodles before he got him. It was as simple as that. He side-stepped Cheyenne and went back to his Glocks. He placed one on his hip and another into the small of his back.

Cheyenne pulled his arm. "Don't you hear me talk-ing to you?"

He jerked away from her. "Yeah, I hear that smoke you blowing, but it's obvious you don't know your brother. That nigga ain't got it all. He never has, and he never will. That fool was gon' let me die on them tracks. The writing is on the wall; it's as simple as that." He pulled on his vest and looked and for a shirt to put on over it.

Cheyenne grabbed him again. "Filipino, look at me. Look at this shit!" She snatched the bandage off of her face and exposed the burned skin. It was pink and peeling. "Can you see this? Look at my face, Filipino."

Filipino turned his eyes from the bed and into her face. He surveyed the wound and felt a pain in his heart. "Damn, Cheyenne." He made a move to touch her cheek, to assess the injury.

She slapped his hand away. "Don't touch me. It's because of you two that shit happened to me. Instead of you two coming together to find out who did this, y'all telling me that you are fighting and trying to kill each other. Really, man?"

Filipino lowered his head. "Baby, you just don't understand. I ain't have nothing against your brother. He taking all of this out of proportion. That nigga almost got me killed tonight. He just stood there and watched a train nearly run me over. That means that he's thinking death and murder, if that's the case, I gotta get the jump on him before he finishes me off. That's how the streets go. You know that." Filipino brushed past her and threw on a shirt. He grabbed his car keys and stopped for look Cheyenne over one last time.

She looked defeated. "So I'm supposed to choose whether I want my neither to remain alive, or my fiancé, the father of my unborn child? What type of shit is that?"

Filipino shrugged his shoulders. "It's the life we live, shawty. I gotta do what I gotta do. I'll see you in a few hours. I swear to God I love you."

Cheyenne rushed him, swinging like a windmill. "You don't fuckin' get it, do you? You think I'm just going to let you go out and kill my brother?" The blows landed all over Filipino's face, busting his lip and popping him in the eye, his cheek, and forehead. More than once he felt the diamond dig into his flesh. She swung harder and harder. "Y'all need to stop this. Grow up. Grow up. Grow up!" Harder and harder the punches landed.

"Get the fuck off of me!" Filipino pushed her with all of his might.

Cheyenne flew backwards and tripped over Filipino's discarded shirt. She lost her balance and the back of her head slammed into the corner of the lamp table, busting it wide open and causing her neck to snap. She was dead before she realized what was happening to her.

Filipino stood at the door, fuming. "You and that nigga got it bad putting y'all hands on me. I ain't wit' that fuck shit. I gotta handle my bidness. You hear me?" he shouted.

He stood there for a minute and looked a little closer. He saw the blood pouring onto her shoulders. Her head bent at a weird angle. The sight spooked him. "Cheyenne? Baby, I'm sorry. Shit. Baby, I'm sorry." He rushed to her side. He picked her up into his arms and laid her on the bed. Her eyes were wide open. He placed a finger to her neck, searching for a pulse. There was none. Now he was really beginning to panic. "Cheyenne? Cheyenne, baby, please come back. I'm sorry," he wailed before falling to his knees.

***

Noodles stood across the street of Combo's mother's home. He downed the rest of the alcohol from his bottle of Patron, broke the bottle on the ground, and wiped his mouth. He was tired of playing games. He wanted to know where Combo was so he could punish him for what he'd done to Cheyenne, and their mother's place of residence. He was tired of losing sleep over the dilemma. The longer he allowed him to remain alive, the more of a threat he caused. It was only a matter of time before he came at his mother, or even Cheyenne again. The next time they might not be so lucky. He crossed the street and jogged up the porch steps, drunk and high as a kite. He rang the doorbell three times and burped. He missed Fancii. For some reason a picture of her came across his mental Rolodex. He shook his head as hard as he could and rang the doorbell again.

"Hold ya horses, hold ya horses," Gia yelled. She had the big cake bowl in her hands, mixing chocolate batter. She stepped up to the door and peeked out of it. She saw the handsome, dark-skinned face of Noodles. He looked familiar. She wondered if he was one of her son Antwan's friends. "Yes, how may I help you?"

Noodles smiled. "Is Combo home?"

She figured he might have been there for him. "No, I'm sorry, baby, but Antwan does not live here."

Noodles grew irritated almost immediately. "Aw, well do you know where he is? He was supposed to help me fix my car, and I ain't been able to get ahold of him." Noodles knew the excuse was lame, but figured he'd try it anyway. Before Combo hit it off as a dope boy, he was known around Crenshaw as a bit of a mechanic. Noodles was sure he probably hadn't touched one to fix in years, but he didn't think his mother knew that.

Gia sighed. "That boy always promising somebody something, and never follows through. He just got a new cell phone. I'll go and get the number off of my refrigerator." Gia was old school. She was still using a cordless phone and had not gotten herself a cell phone as of yet. She turned to go and grab the number.

Noodles tapped on the window. "Ma'am, I gotta use the bathroom too. I been holding it all the way since the bus ride over here." He rocked from left to right to emphasize his point.

Gia laughed. "Boy, my son just got you all screwed up, huh?" She unlocked the door and pushed it open. "Go on 'head, the bathroom is in the back, to the left of the kitchen." She pointed. "Actually, I can show you because his cell number is on the refrigerator. Come on."

Noodles sized her up and smiled. She was 5'6" tall, 140 pounds, caramel-skinned, forty-eight years old. She looked good to him, and oddly familiar. Before he could ask her where it was that he'd seen her before, she brought it up.

"Baby, did you by any chance used to attend Pastor Ryan's church?" she asked, smiling with dimples on both cheeks.

Noodles nodded. "Yeah, when I was a shawty. That was a million years ago. Look, we got a problem." Noodles pulled a Nine out of the small of his back. He aimed it at her.

Gia jumped back and held her hands at shoulder length. "Oh my God. Please don't shoot. I don't have but a little money in here, baby. All that I have you can take though."

Noodles shook his head. "Nall, this ain't about no money. I need you to tell me where Combo is. He been doing a lot of foul shit, and his sins need to catch up with him. Where is he at?" Noodles grabbed her and slammed her into the refrigerator.

Gia's back hit it hard. She closed her eyes and slowly opened them. "Listen, I don't know what transgressions my son has sinned against you, but it has nothing to do with me. Now it's like I said, he isn't here. This is not his house. It's mine."

Noodles grabbed her chin and squeezed it as hard as he could. She groaned out in excruciating pain. "Bitch, listen to me. Your son done burned down my mother's house and shot it up. In the process, he has scarred my sister forever. He been trying to kill my loved ones for the last few months, targeting everybody with no remorse. What is good for the goose is good for the gander. That means that every ounce of pain that he's inflicted on my people, I intend to inflict on his. So I'ma ask you one more time, where is your son?"

***

Filipino knelt in front of Cheyenne and allowed for the tears to sail down his face. There was a huge puddle of blood formed around her body. His knees sank into the carpet because of the blood having drenched it. He shook his head from side to side. "Damn, I'm so sorry, Cheyenne. I'm so sorry, baby." He picked her up and carried her into the bathroom. He placed her into the bathtub and sat on the floor. He didn't know what to do. What to think. His mind was spinning at such a fast pace that it made him dizzy.

There was a knock on the hotel room door. The couple directly underneath their room noticed the red substance leaking from the ceiling and reported it to the manager. The manager was set to get to the bottom of things. He knocked on the door again, this time more aggressively. After getting no response, he took his master key card out of his wallet, slid it into the reader, and waited until it turned green. He pushed opened the door and stepped inside. "Hello, is anybody here?" The manager caught sight of all of the blood and gasped.

Filipino stood up and ran out of the bathroom. Before the man could make it back out of the door, he grabbed him around the neck and pulled him back inside. He flung him to the floor.

The manager scooted backwards on his backside. "Look, man, I didn't see anything. I swear, I won't say a word. Just please don't hurt me."

"We were arguing, and I pushed her. I-I-I didn't mean to push her so hard, but I did. I mean, she was hitting me, and punching me all hard and shit and I should have been able to take it but, she fell, and hit her head. I love this woman, I-I-I just…"

The manager nodded with his hands held out in front of him. "Look, it's not your fault. We can explain this to the authorities and go from there. You tell them what you just told me, and they will have no problem seeing this as an accident. I mean, that's all it is, right?" He made it to his feet.

"That's it. I would never hurt Cheyenne. I love her too much. She's all I think about. All I care about. You have to believe me, Cuz. She had my baby inside of her." Filipino was on the verge of losing his mind.

The manager eased his always toward the door. He thought that if he could get close enough that he could make it out into the hallway where he could holler for help. To him, it was obvious what had taken place. He felt that Filipino had snapped and killed Cheyenne in a lover's spat. It was Los Angeles and wouldn't have been out of the ordinary. He simply wanted no part of it. He was wishing that he'd never stepped foot inside of the room without back up. "Say, buddy, why don't we go for help? The sooner we contact somebody, the faster we can get this unfortunate situation under control." He looked past Filipino's shoulders and saw Cheyenne's hand and arm hanging over the rim of the tub. This terrified him.

Filipino rubbed his face and hollered into his hand. He pulled the Glock from his waistband and aimed at the manager. "I didn't do it on purpose. I swear I didn't." He let go three quick shots into the man's forehead and ran back into the bathroom. He kissed Cheyenne on the cheeks. "I love you, baby. I will always love you, and I am so, so sorry." He grabbed his suitcase of guns, his bulletproof vests, and rushed out of the hotel by use of the back fire escape.

***

Noodles wiped the sweat from the side of his face. He stood in front of Gia with a steak knife in his hand. He had her hands tied behind her back and her ankles bound as well. They were downstairs in her basement. The washing machine continued to wash the load that she'd originally placed inside of it. Noodles had started it over twice while they were waiting for Combo to show up.

Gia groaned into the duct tape. She wanted to see if she could talk some sense into the brute. She was starting to feel guilty about talking her son to walking to his own death.

Noodles ripped the tape partway off of her mouth. "What's up, lady?"

Gia smacked her lips. She tried to swallow her spit, but her throat was so dry that it was nearly impossible. "Son, please. Won't you think about what you're getting ready to do? You're about to take my child's life. My only child. Please don't do this to me."

Noodles knelt down in front of her. He rubbed the side of her face. "Listen to me, ma'am, you are lucky that my heart isn't as cold as your son's. If it was, you would have been gone a long time ago. I'm going to re-pay him an eye for an eye. He hurt my sister, so I'm going to hurt him, and leave it at that. Now do me a fa-vor and shut up before things get real tricky. You feel me?" He slapped the tape back around her mouth and stood up. He could already taste Combo's kill. He was fiending for it.

***

Combo pulled in front of his mother's home and threw the car in park. He looked to Sky, who sat in the passenger's seat. "Look, I'm about to go in here and hol-ler at my mother real quick. Drive this whip up the block and park it. I got all types of enemies and shit. I can't have nobody spotting my whip and airing this bitch out. You know how this shit go. When I come from out of here you about to show me where that fool Noodles lay-ing his head, right?"

Sky nodded. "Yep, long as you wipe our slate clean, I'ma show you where he, Filipino, and Cheyenne laying low. You take care of them and let me go about my bid-ness. Cool?"

Combo smiled. "Cool, shawty. I'll be right back." He kissed her lips and hopped out of the car. He made his way up the stairs and rang the doorbell twice. He tried the knob and was amazed to find that it opened. He pushed it in.

"Mama, where you at? I'm here."

Hood Rich

Chapter 17

Combo opened the door wider and stuck his head inside of his mother's home. He sniffed the air and smelled the fragrance of his mother's perfume. That made him smile. "Mama, where you at, in the bathroom or somethin'?" he asked stepping all the way inside and closing the door behind him.

Gia struggled against her bonds. Tears ran down her eyes. She screamed into the duct tape, but it was of no use. Noodles had stuffed a towel into her mouth before taping her lips again. She needed to warn her son of the impending danger. She wanted to tell him to get out of the house before it was too late.

Combo kicked off his Nike's at the door and stepped onto his mother's soft white carpet. He looked left and saw the Tyler Perry movie playing on her flat-screened television. On the table was a glass of wine, half filled, and a box of tissues. He was accustomed to her movie nights. Over the years she'd often picked two days out of the week where she'd picked a movie to kick back and cry to while she sipped wine. He figured that this night was another one of those nights. He stepped into the front room, picked up the glass of wine, and took a sip out of it. He swished the liquid around in his mouth and swallowed it. He stood there for a moment and frowned his face. "Mama, where are you?"

Noodles stepped out of the closet and into the front room with three strides. He pressed the silenced .45 to the back of Combo's head and cocked the hammer. "I'm right here, son." He purposely made his voice high before curling his lip. "You wanna find a nigga at his

159

weakest, softest moment, you catch him at his mama's house. Long time no muthafuckin' see."

Combo closed his eyes. He couldn't place the voice, but he could already imagine that it was one of the pair. It was either Noodles or Filipino. He was sure of it. Instead of Sky helping to set one of the other men up, he was sure that she had set him up. *Damn, you can't trust them bitches*, he thought. "Say, man, I don't know who you are, or what bidness you want wit' me, but I got two hundred G's stashed here. You can have every penny if you let me up out of this jam. I ain't even gotta see your face." Combo was willing to bargain however he needed to in order to break free of the situation. The truth was that had had stashed five hundred thousand in cash at his mother's home, but he wasn't willing to forgo all of the cash. Two hundred thousand was good money to any robber. He hopped that this was all it was about.

Noodles stepped behind him and wrapped his arm around his neck. He pressed the gun to his temple. "Bitch nigga, if you move in even the slightest I'ma splash yo' Ramen all over the fuckin' floor. Now let me guide you. It's sad that you ain't even asked if your mother was okay one time. You a trifling-ass nigga. All you care about is you. Come on." Noodles grabbed him aggressively and guided him toward the back of the house. Once there he took him down the back steps and into the basement. He threw him on the floor in front of his bound mother.

Gia jumped up and down in her chair as best she could. She screamed into the tape, calling her son's name. She wanted Noodles to take her out, to save her son. He had his whole life ahead of him, she felt. She would be his sacrifice.

Noodles mugged Combo and aimed his gun at him. "You see that chair right there? Sit yo' punk ass in it and be still."

Combo slowly made his way to the empty chair and took a seat. After confirming that the invader was Noodles, a chill came over his body. He felt as if the angel of death was in the house. His odds of survival were slim, at best. He knew this. "Look, Noodles, man, let's squash this shit. All this killing going in is ridiculous. We gotta do better for the community, bruh. Better for ourselves. Better for our family. It's time we make a change."

Noodles aimed and fired.

Boof. The bullet pierced into Combo's shoulder and knocked a chunk out of it. He flew off of the chair and wound up on his back on the ground with blood gushing out of him. His shoulder felt as if it were on fire. He kicked his legs wildly and placed his hand over the wound. Blood gushed through his fingers and dropped off of his wrist.

"You talking all that positive shit now? Huh? Nigga, it's way too late for that. You done killed my man's mother, hit him up, scarred my sister, and we ain't even gon' talk about what you did to me."

Boof. Fire spit from the gun again. The bullet knocked a hole into Combo's thigh.

Combo grabbed it and scooted all the way back against the washing machine. Sweat poured off of his forehead. It ran down his neck and into his shirt, where he was wearing a bullet proof vest. He raised a hand. "Noodles. Come on, man. Now we even. We even, homeboy. I ain't never killed nobody you fuck wit'. The whole fire thing was just to send a warning. I ain't know yo' sister was up in there. I swear to God, I didn't know Cheyenne was there."

At the mention of Cheyenne's name, Noodles froze in place. He tightened his grip around the gun. He imagined how Cheyenne's burn scars had looked the last time he'd seen her. This made his heart heavy. His sister was his heart and soul. Noodles replaced his guns and grabbed the butcher's knife from the top of the dryer. He pointed at Combo with it. "You scarred Cheyenne for life, homie.

Every time she looks in the mirror for the rest of her life she's going to have to deal with her reflection, and that's all because of what you did to her. You ain't nothing but a coward. Through and through." He stepped beside Gia and held the knife to her cheek. "What if I did that shit to your mother, homie? Huh? What if I did some shit like this? If I took this knife, and sawed off a piece of your mother's cheek?" Noodles poked the knife into Gia's cheek and sliced downward. He pulled at the flesh until he was able to get a nice amount of it and cut through a small portion.

Gia screamed. She blew snot out of her nose. Her eyes were big as saucers. Tears sailed down her cheeks. She could feel the blade cutting away a piece of her. It hurt so bad that she peed a little.

Noodles, out of his mind, held the piece of cheek in his hand, and tossed it on to Combo's chest. "I love my muthafuckin' sister, nigga. I love my sister, and I love my mother. If a ma'fucka hurt them like you did, boy, I'm just gon' show you better than I can tell you." He placed the knife back on the dryer and pulled out the .45 again. He aimed and fired another shot through Combo's knee, knocking it off of his leg.

Combo rolled away and shot up. He limped as fast as he could to the stairs. He tried to ascend them and caught two more bullets to the back of his thighs. The bullets burned through his tissues and dropped him to the ground. He fell on the first step, helpless. Blood leaked out of him like a broken pipe.

Noodles grabbed him by the hair and pulled him back down into the basement. He dragged him in front of Gia and dropped him. He walked over and took the butcher's knife off of the dryer.

Combo groaned and cried tears of pain. "Noodles, just take the two hundred thousand. Take the money and go. Please. It's in my mother's bedroom. Way back in her closet. She knows the combination. Please, man. I'm sorry for what I did to your people. Sorry for what I did to you."

Noodles slashed him across the face three times with lightning speed. Then he raised the knife and slammed it into his shoulder, directly in the center of his bullet wound. He twisted it.

"Argh!" Combo humped into the air and twisted on his side.

Noodles looked him over. He felt sick to his stomach. For him, Combo represented all of the pain and strife that he'd experienced over the last few months. He wished that he could have caused him more pain.

Gia's cheek bled profusely. She kept her eyes open. Something in her soul told her that this might have been the last time that she was going to see her son alive. She silently prayed for deliverance, prayed for them to be saved. From what she could hear, she knew that Combo had done wrong, but what they were experiencing seemed more than enough for payment.

Noodles grabbed the knife out of Combo and slashed his face again. He stood back and dropped the knife on the floor. "Gia, nod your head if you really know where this money is that he's talking about? Do you know?" Noodles hollered.

Gia swallowed her spit and nodded.

Noodles kicked Combo in the ass hard. "How much is it again?"

Combo groaned. "Two hundred bands. Two hundred. You can have that shit. Just let my mama get me to a hospital."

"A hospital? Nigga." Noodles stood over him and aimed for his face.

Boof. Boof. Boof. Boof.

Gia screamed as loud as she could as she watched bullet after bullet knock away Combo's facial features until he was left in a bloody heap with eyes wide open.

Noodles grabbed her by the hair and dragged her up the stairs and to her room. He recovered the money and blazed her with three slugs before leaving through the back door.

***

Filipino stormed into the mansion with his head down. He was hot and sweaty. He felt like he was losing his mind. Bronco could tell that something was wrong. He'd not spoken the entire drive back to his home. He headed straight down the long hallway that led to Bronco's office. Once there, he slumped on the couch.

Bronco stepped in and closed the door. He took a seat behind his desk and grabbed a cigar out of the box, cut the end, and set it ablaze. After three puffs, he blew the smoke toward the ceiling. "Filipino, what's the matter?"

Filipino was near tears again. "Look, man, I need to holler at my sister. I know she's here. Don't tell me she's not here. I need to talk to her right now, I'm not fucking playing."

Bronco lowered his eyes and held up a hand. "Okay, okay, son. Calm down. What do you need to speak with her about?"

Filipino hopped up. "Don't worry about it. Just get her down here to me right now. I need to see her, man. Please. I need my sister."

Bronco nodded. "Okay, okay." He got up and stepped out of the room. He closed the door and walked down the hallway, and up the stairs headed toward the west wing of the mansion when he bumped into Mills coming out of the wine cellar. "Son, just the man I was hoping to see."

Mills was riled up. Fancii had just finished giving him some of the best head of his young life. He had a strong urge for red wine. After grabbing the bottle, he intended on going back to the room where he would party with Fancii until the sun rose. "What's up, Dad?"

"We seem to have a bit of a situation that I need your help with. Well, not actually your help, but Fancii's. You see, her brother is down the way there, and he says he really needs to speak with her. Now I got him in control of some very important things, and I need his head on straight. You gotta get him to talk to her."

Mills scoffed. He was disgusted. "You allowed for one of those ghetto low lives to come into our home? Are you out of your fuckin' mind? Don't you understand that we'll have to move now?"

It took all of the strength in the world for Bronco to not punch him directly in the mouth. The way Mills spoke to him agitated him in the worst way. "Mills, now I done told yo' ass about coming at me with that tone of voice. This is my house, and you'll respect me in it. I can let in whoever I want to because I own this property. You got that?"

Mills sucked his teeth. "I don't care about none of that. You're putting our entire family at risk with these moronic antics of yours. What does he need to speak with her about?"

Filipino stepped out of the shadows. "Punk-ass rich boy, don't worry about it. Just go and get my sister, or it's gon' be a major problem in this ma'fucka. You ain't supposed to be holding her hostage no muthafuckin' way. I don't know who you think you are."

Mills stepped past Bronco and poked his chest out. He was high off of two Percocets and Patron. He felt more courage than he would have usually had. "This is what I'm talking about. You let one of them thugs into our home, and we're forced to go through some shit like this. I don't know where you had this peasant waiting but send him back there. I'll send Fancii to him when I'm done with her." He turned his nose up at him. He was about to walk past him when Filipino knocked the bottle of wine out of his hand and pushed him as hard as he could. Mills flew backward into the wall. The picture of Barack Obama fell from its place and landed on top of his head.

"Nigga, I don't know who the fuck you talking to, but it ain't sweet. I don't give a damn who you are. I'll smoke yo' punk ass in this house right now." He pulled a Glock out of his waist and cocked it.

"Whoa. Whoa. Whoa." Bronco jumped in front of Filipino and held his hands up. "Chill out, Filipino. That's my son."

"I don't give a fuck who he is. He talking that tough shit, he can catch a few of these hot ones like everybody else. These bullets don't gives fuck if he rich or poor, they'll send him to where he wanna be. Trust me on that."

Mills climbed to his feet and flared his nostrils. "That's all you hoodlums care about is guns. Take them away from you, and you wouldn't know what to do."

Fancii poked her head out of the room. "I thought I heard your voice, Filipino. What are you doing here?"

Hood Rich

Chapter 18

Filipino paced back and forth in front of Fancii. He couldn't help but notice that she looked much skinnier then the last time he'd seen her. She looked more fragile as well. Her cheekbones were prominent. Her crossed thighs were slimmer. She wiped her nose with the back of her hand. She shook as if she was cold. "Filipino, what is the matter, little brother? You're freaking me out right now."

Unbeknownst to them, Eliza had left her cell phone in the room under the couch. She wanted to make sure that she recorded their conversation. Just like she'd surmised before, there was bound to be something that popped up she could use.

Filipino blinked tears and wiped his face. "Look, I'm about to tell you something, and I don't want you to freak out like you've been talking about, or for you to lose your mind. I need a shoulder right now. I need your undying love and support."

Fancii nodded. She couldn't fathom what the big deal could be. They had already been through so much over the last few months. She knew that he'd done a lot of crazy things: murdered people, robbed them, and all kinds of other stuff, and he'd confessed them to her. This had been the first time that she'd witnessed him acting the way that he currently was. "Just tell me what's going on, Filipino. Please. I'm here for you. I love you. We are all we have left."

Filipino squeezed his eyelids together tightly. Tears sailed down his cheeks. "Damn, Fancii, I killed her. I didn't mean to, but I killed her, and now she's just gone.

The love of my life is gone." He fell to his knees and put his head in her lap.

Fancii was confused. She sniffed snot back into her nose and swallowed it. "Who did you kill, Filipino? And how?"

Filipino was taking it hard. He felt his stomach turning into knots. He remembered how Cheyenne had looked bleeding profusely in the bathtub with her neck bent at an awkward angle. He shook his head, pained. Thought about their last lovemaking session. How she felt in his arms. Her moans. Her kisses. All of the memories hurt him to the very core.

"Who, Filipino? Do I know her?"

He nodded, and more tears dripped off of his chin. "Cheyenne. She's dead."

Fancii hopped up with her eyes bucked. "Cheyenne? You killed Cheyenne?"

He was too weak to tell her to shut the fuck up. Instead, he nodded and crouched over, sobbing. His head shook from side to side. "I didn't mean to. We were arguing about that nigga Noodles. Earlier that night, me and him had gotten into a huge fight because he found out that I was fucking Cheyenne behind his back and had gotten her pregnant. He says I betrayed him. That I broke our bonds. We fought on the railroads tracks behind the glass factory. That nigga got the best of me. My mind was all over the place." More sobbing. "He whooped me and wound up knocking me out, left me in the middle of the train tracks with a train burrowing down on me. Had the horn of the locomotive not sounded, I would have been run over and crushed to death. I woke up in the nick of time. Long story short, when I got back to the telly, I told Cheyenne what I was about to do to Noodles. Told her I was finna kill his ass. She wasn't trying to hear that. She attacked me, swinging all wild and shit. Her punches got to fuckin' me up, so I pushed her hard. She flew back and hit her head on the corner of the table and snapped her neck during her landing. I couldn't save her. I wanted to, but by the time I got to her side, she was already dead. My baby gone, her and my seed." He planted his face on the carpet and broke all the way down.

Fancii's high was blown. She couldn't believe what she was hearing. She and Cheyenne had been the best of friends ever since they were in elementary school. The fact that she was gone was devastating, and even worse, her brother Filipino had been the one to kill her.

"Say something, Fancii. I need you right now. Tell me something. Please." He rocked back and forth on his knees. The Velcro of his bulletproof vest sounded.

Fancii knelt on her knees and rubbed his big back. "It's okay, Filipino. It's okay, bro, we're going to get through this. We just have to remain calm." Those were the words that came out of her mouth, but deep down, she was torn up. When it came to Crenshaw, it seemed that it was always nothing more than war and devastation. Funeral after funeral. She was tired of the chaos. It only heightened her reasons for wanting to stay in Bel-Air, away from the Black, Latino, and underprivileged people. In Bel-Air, she never had to worry about the negative life-altering things that Crenshaw had offer on a day-to-day basis. From Bel-Air, she could see her dreams becoming reality. Role models surrounded her on a daily basis. She was able to see success, so she kept success on her mind at all times. "Does Noodles know?"

Filipino jumped up and wiped his face. He sniffed and swallowed the lump of mucus in his throat. Sighed. "Nall, he don't know yet, but I ain't about to keep this shit from him. I'ma holler at him in person and let him know what it is." Filipino knew that things couldn't end well. But if similar things had taken place with Fancii, he would have wanted for his right hand to tell him what it was. He wasn't sure how he'd react, but he definitely would have given him credit for coming clean.

Fancii stood and shook her head. "No, Filipino. You can't do that. You should already know that as soon as you tell Noodles what it is, he's going to kill you, or you're going to kill him. Either way, things won't be good. You need to sleep on this for a few days. Think it through more thoroughly. Where is Cheyenne's body now?"

He shrugged his shoulders. "I don't know. I left her in the hotel in the bathroom. Her and the hotel manager. Dude stumbled in at the wrong time, so he had to get what he had coming to him."

Fancii's mouth dropped wide open. "Damn, so you iced two people in the same night?" She was blown away. "What's the matter with you?" She grabbed him by the shirt and smacked him.

Filipino took the blow as a show of discipline. "I don't know, Sis, I been fucking up. What am I going to do? What am I going to do?" he repeated, falling to his knees.

Fancii was disgusted. She grabbed his arm and pulled him up. "Get yo' ass up. I don't know what all of this crying and sobbing shit is about but knock it off. You did what you did, now it's time to man up. You have to get the hell out of town. Seriously. Once Noodles finds out, it's going to be hell to pay the Captain."

Filipino knocked her hand away. "Fuck Noodles. He the reason all of this shit happened. I don't give a fuck about him finding out. In fact, I'ma find him to show you muthafuckas that I ain't afraid."

Fancii stepped into his face. "And then what, huh? I lose my mother, one of my best friends, and my brother all in the same year? Happy 20-muthafuckin'-19 to me, huh?"

Filipino moved her out of the way. "It's not about you right now, Fancii. It's about me, and what I've done. You can stay here in your precious Bel-Air. Act like the hood don't exist anymore. Live in your fuckin' fantasy world. I got a lot of work to do. If I never see you again, I just want you to know that I love you." He kissed her and stormed out of the door.

Fancii stood with her head down, lost and confused.

***

Sondra stepped out of the hotel bathroom and covered her mouth with her hand. "Oh by fuckin God, Nadell, what is all this?" Her eyes searched the bed. She was in complete and utter shock.

Noodles threw the last stack of cash on to the bed. The entire king-sized mattress was covered with money. The bundles had rubber bands over them. "This five hundred thousand dollars, Mama. This is your money. It belongs to you. I want you to take it, and I'ma roll you over to Seattle, where you can get a place and chill for a few months while I work on getting your papers approved."

Sondra looked over the bed again. It was the most money she'd ever seen in her entire life. "Baby, what have you done? Whose money is this?" She stepped forward and stood beside him.

"It's yours. I already told you that. It all belongs to you. That's all you need to know." Noodles took the cash and stuffed the duffel bag with it. After filling it with the contents, he zipped it up and dropped it next to her foot. "Come on, it's time to get you dressed." He opened the closet door and pulled out a random outfit.

Sondra sat on the bed and covered her face with her hands. Tears seeped out of her eyes. She felt deep within her soul that something was wrong. "Nadell, I need you to talk to me. Tell me what is going on." She uncovered her face and looked him over.

Noodles balled his face. "Why something gotta be wrong, Queen? Why you just can't listen to what I'm saying, and do like I say? Huh, Mama?"

"Because I ain't never been no damn fool, that's why. Now tell me what the hell is going on!" She stood up and grabbed his chin with one hand. She peered into his eyes, searching.

Noodles held his composure. This was his mother. His queen. The love of his life. The person he worshipped more than anyone else on earth. "Mama, I love you, and there is nothing wrong. I need for you to get dressed so we can get out of here." He removed her hands from his face, kissed the palms of them. "Come on now."

Sondra stepped away from him and picked up the outfit that he'd placed out for her. She removed her robe and allowed for it to drop to the floor. She turned her back to him and held the pants, ready to put them on, then dropped them. She shook her head again and faced Noodles. "Who am I to you, Nadell, huh? Am I your woman, or your mother?" She stepped into his faces and made him wrap his arm around her lower back.

Noodles was taken aback. "What?"

"You heard me. You're bringing me large sums of money. Got me waiting around in a hotel for you scantily clad. I can't go nowhere without your permission. I can't do nothing without your permission. You pretty much run the entire show, so I can't be your mother. If I'm not your mother, you must think that I am your woman, so what do you wanna do? Huh? I'm already in my bra and panties. You want me, take me right now, Nadell." She grabbed his other hand and pulled him closer to her. Her forehead rested on his.

Noodles closed his eyes and slowly opened them. Her brown ones peered into his own. He could smell the scent of her perfume. "Mama, I don't know what has gotten into you, but you're tripping right now. I need for you to get dressed so we can go."

She stepped back and opened her bra in the front. Her breasts spilled out of the cups. Noodles saw the round areolas and covered them with his big hands. "Whoa, Mama, what the fuck are you doing?"

"Take me, Nadell. I'm tired of you ruling me! I'm supposed to be mother, yet you're always telling me what to do and when to do it. I feel like the child instead of the parent. Nall, scratch that, I feel like your woman. Since that's the case, let's nip this shit in the bud right here, and right now. Now what do you want to do?" She stepped back three feet and stood before him.

Noodles sized her up quickly and looked off. "Put your bra back on, Mama." He turned his back to her.

"I'm sorry. I didn't mean to make you feel less than a Queen. I just wanted to get you out of this corrupt-ass city. I love you, and you're the most important person to me outside of Cheyenne." He turned around and pulled her into his arms. "Seriously, I'm sorry, Mama."

She hugged him back. She took a deep breath and exhaled. "It's okay, baby. I know you are. I just wish you would give me more leeway. Don't be so controlling all the time. You know that you're the only man in my life. You ain't gotta remind yourself of your authority every single day." She picked up her bra and replaced it over her body. "Now we can go wherever you wanna go, but tell me the truth about this money, and why you want me out of the city. Can you do that?"

Noodles nodded, and read the text on his phone. It was from Sky. It read: "They just found Cheyenne dead in a hotel bathtub. I'm texting you the information right now."

Noodles dropped the phone and fell to his knees.

Chapter 19

Fancii stepped forward and dropped a rose into Cheyenne's grave. She wiped a sole tear from her eye and said a short prayer just as the rain began to descend from the sky. She flipped out her umbrella and held it over her head. After saying her short prayer, she walked up to Sondra and hugged her. "Mama, I'm so sorry for your loss. All of this senseless killing is getting ridiculous. I can only hope that they find the perpetrator."

Sondra hugged her back weakly. "Thank you for your empathy, baby. You were always a great friend to my daughter. I can let you know firsthand that she really appreciated you. I hope that you get as far away from this Crenshaw life as you possibly can. And eat a sandwich or something. You're getting skinnier by the day." She hugged her and kissed both of her cheeks.

Fancii hugged her back and stepped away from the ceremony. Mills awaited her inside of the limousine. She was more than halfway there when Noodles stepped from behind a tree dressed in all black, with sunglasses cover-ing his eyes. Fancii nearly jumped out of her skin. "Jeez, you scared the shit out of me."

Noodles stood there. Rain popped off of his black L.A. fitted cap. "That's my bad. I ain't mean to do that." He felt emotional at the sight of her.

Fancii looked over his shoulders and to the parking lot. Mills stepped out of the limousine and waved her over. She cleared her throat. "I'm sorry for your loss, Noodles. I know that Cheyenne meant the world to you. How are you holding up?"

Noodles looked over to his sister's grave and dropped two tears. "Day by day, Fancii. That's all I can do." He saw Sondra kneel in front of the grave and break all the way down. She wailed the word "no" as loud as she could. "Have you seen or heard from Filipino?"

"Nall, not since last week. But you know I'm always working. I'm trying to get onto the next chapter of my life. You know how that goes." She shifted uncomfortably.

Mills beeped the horn and slapped the top of the limousine's hood. "Fancii let's go. Damn!" he yelled, grow-ing impatient.

"I'm coming, Mills. Chill out! Jesus!" she shouted back at him.

"Yeah, shut the fuck up, rich boy!" Noodles snapped, ready to smoke his ass. "She'll be over there in a minute.

Fancii felt some type of way. She didn't want things to progress. She knew how Noodles was when he was upset. He would murder with no afterthought. "Look, Noodles, maybe I should get out of here. I am sorry for your loss, and I still love you. That will never change." She hugged him.

Noodles wiped his tears away. "They say your brother killed my sister. You know anything about that?"

Fancii froze in place. "What? No, of course not. Why would Filipino do anything like that? He loved her, and plus she was pregnant with his kid. That makes no sense."

"Probably because I whooped his ass the same night that all of that took place. That nigga couldn't fuck wit' my bidness, so he took that shit out on my sister. You know how most cowards get down. I mean, after all, he is your blood."

Fancii took the shot personally, but still chose to take the high road. There was no sense in arguing with Noo-dles when he was angry. He only looked for a reason to further infuriate himself. When he got as mad as he possibly could, then bodies began to drop. It was classic him. "You know what, Noodles? Like I said, I'm sorry for your loss, and I wish you the best." She attempted to walk around him.

Noodles blocked her path. "Fancii, I will always love you, girl, but I swear to God that if your brother don't come out of hiding soon, I'ma be forced to turn into a coward like him and take my anger out on the ma'fuckas that mean the most to him. It won't be no hard feelings, just war of the streets." He bumped her hard enough to knock her backward and kept going. He knelt beside his mother and comforted her.

Filipino looked on from a far distance. At the sight of Noodles bumping Fancii out of the way he wanted to pick up his gun and empty the clip into Noodles. The only reason he let it slide was because of the setting. Had he killed him, he would have had to kill everyone present.

***

Fancii eased into the limousine and placed the seatbelt around herself. She closed her eyes and tried to think positive thoughts. After Cheyenne's funeral, she did not see any reason for her to come anywhere near Crenshaw again. She'd made up her mind.

Mills got into the limousine and slammed the door hard. "Drive off!" he hollered, and then rolled up the partition. The stretch Navigator lurched forward and took off from the curb. He turned up the music. He faced Fancii, cocked back, and punched her in the jaw as hard as he could before pulling her onto the ground and straddling her. He slapped her across the face. "I told you, bitch." Slap. "I told you about disrespecting me." Another slap.

Fancii received the blows and laid still. She didn't want to fight, didn't want to give him any reason to send her back to Crenshaw. "I'm sorry, Mills. I'm sorry. I swear I won't do it again."

"Oh, I know you won't, you diseased peasant." He pulled the letter from the clinic out of his inside coat pocket and smashed it into her face. "You gave me this ghetto shit. Bitch, you did this." He stuffed the letter into her mouth and beat on the partition.

The driver lowered it. "Sir, may I help you?"

"Stop this muthafucka right now. This bitch getting out!" He slapped her again.

The driver stepped on the brakes. He got out of the truck and opened the back door. He stepped to the side as the rain picked up its velocity.

Mills pulled Fancii out of the limo while she kicked and screamed, then dumped her in the road. He kicked her as hard he could in the stomach. She threw up her breakfast and rolled three feet. He threw the letter from the clinic at her and got back into his limo. He placed an ounce of China White inside of her purse, tossed it to her, and then ordered the driver to pull off.

Fancii crawled a short distance and fell on her stomach. She was out of breath. She curled into a ball after grabbing the paper. She read over its contents. When she came to the section that told her that Mills was HIV positive, she jumped up and took off running down the road, screaming in tears. She ran a quarter mile before slumping to her knees and crying her heart out in the middle of the road.

***

Noodles held Sondra under his left arm while he pushed his whip. The Boys II Men song "It's So Hard To Say Goodbye" crooned out of the speakers. He was going over the multiple memories of Cheyenne in his head when he saw Fancii on the side of the road, laid out flat on her stomach. He slammed on the brakes and jumped out of the car after throwing it in park. When he got to her side, he saw her purse lying next to her. All of its contents were everywhere. He rolled her over. Her eyes were closed. White foam oozed out of her mouth. In her right forearm was a syringe. He touched the side of her neck and checked for a pulse. Felt none. He yanked the syringe out and saw that the entire area was full of needle pricks. He held her in his arms.

"Aw shit, Fancii, what the fuck is going on?" he hollered. He laid her on her back and began to do CPR. "Come on, Fancii. Come on, baby. Please." More chest compressions. He tried and tried, but it was of no use. Fancii was no longer living. Her soul stood across the street safely, watching Noodles trying to revive her body. After watching him for ten minutes, she turned her back on him and walked down the road.

Sondra stood on side of the front passenger door, shedding tears of sorrow for Fancii. She'd watched her grow into a woman and begin to chase her dreams. It was funny how life worked, she thought. Just when you thought you were on your way, the angel of death could make an appearance out of nowhere. Life was unfair, she thought.

Noodles shed tears and gave up after seeing that he was fighting a lost cause. He picked up her body and carried her to the car. "Mama, open the back door. Open the back door and let me get her inside please. We gotta get her to a hospital right away."

Sondra rushed around and slipped when she got to the back of the car. The rain began to pour more heavily. She slowly came to her feet. Her knees were bloodied. "Damn, look what I did."

Noodles adjusted Fancii in his arms. "Mama, come on, this girl getting heavy."

***

Filipino was flying down the long road in his Ducati. On each side of him were trees. He felt an eerie feeling traveling down the path while it rained and thunderstormed. He twisted the handle to increase his speeds and allowed the wind and rain to course against his helmet. He'd said his final goodbyes to Cheyenne. Now it was time to find Noodles so they could settle things once and for all. The engine roared. He slowed and winded the road. He looked ahead to see a car parked in the middle of the street. His maximum speeds allowed him to cover the distance quickly. When he got close enough to make out the pair of Sondra and Noodles, he slowed the bike. When he saw Noodles carrying a limp Fancii, his heart leaped in his chest. Noodles struggled to get Fancii into the back of the car.

Filipino slowed his bike, brought it to a halt, and hopped off of it. He pulled two Forty Glocks from his hips and hollered, "Aye! Noodles! What the fuck y'all doing wit' my sister?"

Sondra waved at him. "Baby, she's dead. We found her on the side of the road. My son didn't - " she began.

"Dead?" Filipino stopped in his tracks and let loose. Boom. Boom. Boom. Boom.

"Shit!" Sondra hopped into the passenger's side and slammed the door.

Noodles dropped Fancii to the pavement and fired back at him. Bocka. Bocka. Bocka.

Filipino took off running into the woods. He hid behind a tree and peeked around it. He aimed at the car again. Boom. Boom. Boom. Both guns jumped in his hands.

The passenger window shattered. The glass landed all over Sondra. She covered her head and screamed. "Noo-dles, get your ass in this car!"

Bocka. Bocka. Bocka. Noodles fired back at Filipino. He threw Fancii into the back seat and slammed the door. Four more bullets crashed into the body of the car before he peeled away from the curb.

Filipino ran back to the road and fired five shots in their direction. He picked up his bike, jumped on it, and sped toward them, picking up ground swiftly. He fired a shot. It shattered the back window.

Noodles ducked down and swerved the car, nearly losing his handle of the wheel. "Fuck, that nigga must think I killed Fancii or something." He stepped on the gas.

"That's probably because of his own guilty conscience of what he did to Cheyenne," Sondra said, ducking as low to the floor as she possibly could.

Noodles increased his speed as he flew out of the arboretum and made a hard right. The car fishtailed. He slammed on the brakes.

Filipino flew out of the arboretum firing.

Boom. Boom. Boom. Boom.

His bullets rocked the car, busting the back passenger window. "Give me my sister! Bitch-ass nigga."

Noodles floored the car again. He looked over his shoulder. Aimed at the busted back window and fired.

Bocka. Bocka. Bocka.

"I'ma kill that nigga, Mama. You know I am."

Sondra's ears were ringing like never before. She was scared for her life. She clasped her fingers together and prayed to Jehovah for His mercy. "Noodles, get us out of here."

Noodles stepped on the gas. The car lurched forward. In the process, Fancii's body flew onto the floor. Noodles checked his rearview mirror. Filipino was gaining speed. Noodles flew through the red light amidst a bunch of horns blowing from the other drivers on the road. He wound up on the highway storming at a hundred miles an hour. The lightning intensified. Water kicked up from the expressway. He could barely see.

Filipino weaved in and out of traffic. He pulled along-side of Sondra's windows and fired into the car. Boom. Boom. Boom.

Noodles swerved and skinned the median. He lost his front bumper. The left headlight was knocked out. He tried to hit Filipino with the car, and it spun out of con-trol. He slammed on the brakes. The car skidded and crashed into the back of a pickup truck, causing it to flip over and over and over and over. Sondra flew out of it and landed in the middle of the highway. A

Volkswagen met her instantly, knocking her fifty feet into the air. She landed on the opposite side of the highway.

The car continued to flip. It stopped and landed upside down. Noodles was trapped. A fire broke out. It singed his clothes. In a matter of seconds, he was on fire, burning and being scalded to death.

Filipino dropped his bike. He jogged over to Sondra and popped her twice facially. He got into a sprint and rushed over to Noodles. He could hear him screaming in the car. The sound delighted him.

Noodles saw Filipino's Jordans standing over the whip. He struggled to break free, but the metal had crunched inward, trapping him in place. He closed his eyes and accepted his fate. Before the car exploded, he heard the sirens approaching, and then he was dead.

Filipino turned around, firing at Twelve.

Boom. Boom. Boom. Boom.

More cars pulled up. They opened their doors, and he knelt down, at the ready. He ducked every time he fired in their direction. It was clear he was on a suicide mission.

Filipino felt he had nothing else to live for. Everybody that he cared about was gone. All of his close family, his right-hand man, and family. It was pointless to be alive. He shot until his clips were empty. As soon as they were, he took off running toward Twelve. They fired immedi-ately. Before he could take ten steps, he was hit more than eighty times. He fell to the ground chest first, a slight smile spread across his face.

To Be Continued…
Street Kings 3
Coming Soon

Submission Guideline

Submit the first three chapters of your completed manuscript to ldpsubmissions@gmail.com, subject line: Your book's title. The manuscript must be in a .doc file and sent as an attachment. Document should be in Times New Roman, double spaced and in size 12 font. Also, provide your synopsis and full contact information. If sending multiple submissions, they must each be in a separate email.

Have a story but no way to send it electronically? You can still submit to LDP/Ca$h Presents. Send in the first three chapters, written or typed, of your completed manuscript to:

LDP: Submissions Dept
Po Box 870494
Mesquite, Tx 75187

DO NOT send original manuscript. Must be a duplicate.

Provide your synopsis and a cover letter containing your full contact information.

Thanks for considering LDP and Ca$h Presents.

Coming Soon from Lock Down Publications/Ca$h Presents

BOW DOWN TO MY GANGSTA

By **Ca$h**

TORN BETWEEN TWO

By **Coffee**

BLOOD STAINS OF A SHOTTA **III**

By **Jamaica**

STEADY MOBBIN **III**

By **Marcellus Allen**

BLOOD OF A BOSS **VI**

By **Askari**

LOYAL TO THE GAME **IV**

LIFE OF SIN **III**

By **T.J. & Jelissa**

A DOPEBOY'S PRAYER **II**

By **Eddie "Wolf" Lee**

IF LOVING YOU IS WRONG… **III**

By **Jelissa**

TRUE SAVAGE **VII**

By **Chris Green**

BLAST FOR ME **III**

DUFFLE BAG CARTEL **IV**

By **Ghost**

ADDICTIED TO THE DRAMA **III**

By **Jamila Mathis**

A HUSTLER'S DECEIT 3

Hood Rich

KILL ZONE **II**

BAE BELONGS TO ME **III**

SOUL OF A MONSTER II

By **Aryanna**

THE COST OF LOYALTY **III**

By **Kweli**

SHE FELL IN LOVE WITH A REAL ONE **II**

By **Tamara Butler**

RENEGADE BOYS **III**

By **Meesha**

A GANGSTER'S SYN II

By **J-Blunt**

KING OF NEW YORK V

RISE TO POWER III

COKE KINGS III

By **T.J. Edwards**

GORILLAZ IN THE BAY IV

De'Kari

THE STREETS ARE CALLING II

Duquie Wilson

KINGPIN KILLAZ IV

STREET KINGS 3

PAID IN BLOOD 2

Hood Rich

SINS OF A HUSTLA II

ASAD

TRIGGADALE III

Street Kings 2

Elijah R. Freeman
MARRIED TO A BOSS III
By Destiny Skai & Chris Green
KINGZ OF THE GAME IV
Playa Ray
SLAUGHTER GANG III
By Willie Slaughter
THE HEART OF A SAVAGE II
By Jibril Williams
FUK SHYT II
By Blakk Diamond
THE DOPEMAN'S BODYGAURD II
By Tranay Adams

Available Now
RESTRAINING ORDER **I & II**
By **CA$H & Coffee**
LOVE KNOWS NO BOUNDARIES **I II & III**
By **Coffee**
RAISED AS A GOON I, II, III & IV
BRED BY THE SLUMS I, II, III
BLAST FOR ME I & II
ROTTEN TO THE CORE I II III
A BRONX TALE I, II, III
DUFFEL BAG CARTEL I II III

189

Hood Rich

By **Ghost**
LAY IT DOWN **I & II**
LAST OF A DYING BREED
BLOOD STAINS OF A SHOTTA I & II
By **Jamaica**
LOYAL TO THE GAME
LOYAL TO THE GAME II
LOYAL TO THE GAME III
LIFE OF SIN I, II
By **TJ & Jelissa**
BLOODY COMMAS I & II
SKI MASK CARTEL I II & III
KING OF NEW YORK I II,III IV
RISE TO POWER I II
COKE KINGS I II
By **T.J. Edwards**
IF LOVING HIM IS WRONG…I & II
LOVE ME EVEN WHEN IT HURTS I II III
By **Jelissa**
WHEN THE STREETS CLAP BACK I & II III
By **Jibril Williams**
A DISTINGUISHED THUG STOLE MY HEART I II & III
LOVE SHOULDN'T HURT I II III IV
RENEGADE BOYS I & II
By **Meesha**
A GANGSTER'S CODE I &, II III
A GANGSTER'S SYN

190

Street Kings 2

By **J-Blunt**
PUSH IT TO THE LIMIT
By **Bre' Hayes**
BLOOD OF A BOSS **I, II, III, IV, V**
By **Askari**
THE STREETS BLEED MURDER **I, II & III**
THE HEART OF A GANGSTA I II& III
By **Jerry Jackson**
CUM FOR ME
CUM FOR ME 2
CUM FOR ME 3
CUM FOR ME 4
CUM FOR ME 5
An **LDP Erotica Collaboration**
BRIDE OF A HUSTLA **I II & II**
THE FETTI GIRLS **I, II& III**
CORRUPTED BY A GANGSTA I, II III, IV
By **Destiny Skai**
WHEN A GOOD GIRL GOES BAD
By **Adrienne**
THE COST OF LOYALTY
By Kweli
A GANGSTER'S REVENGE **I II III & IV**
THE BOSS MAN'S DAUGHTERS
THE BOSS MAN'S DAUGHTERS II
THE BOSSMAN'S DAUGHTERS III
THE BOSSMAN'S DAUGHTERS IV

Hood Rich

THE BOSS MAN'S DAUGHTERS **V**

A SAVAGE LOVE **I & II**

BAE BELONGS TO ME I II

A HUSTLER'S DECEIT I, II, III

WHAT BAD BITCHES DO I, II, III

SOUL OF A MONSTER

By **Aryanna**

A KINGPIN'S AMBITON

A KINGPIN'S AMBITION **II**

I MURDER FOR THE DOUGH

By **Ambitious**

TRUE SAVAGE

TRUE SAVAGE II

TRUE SAVAGE **III**

TRUE SAVAGE **IV**

TRUE SAVAGE **V**

TRUE SAVAGE **VI**

By **Chris Green**

A DOPEBOY'S PRAYER

By **Eddie "Wolf" Lee**

THE KING CARTEL **I, II & III**

By **Frank Gresham**

THESE NIGGAS AIN'T LOYAL **I, II & III**

By **Nikki Tee**

GANGSTA SHYT **I II &III**

By **CATO**

THE ULTIMATE BETRAYAL

By **Phoenix**

BOSS'N UP **I , II & III**

By **Royal Nicole**

I LOVE YOU TO DEATH

By **Destiny J**

I RIDE FOR MY HITTA

I STILL RIDE FOR MY HITTA

By **Misty Holt**

LOVE & CHASIN' PAPER

By **Qay Crockett**

TO DIE IN VAIN

SINS OF A HUSTLA

By **ASAD**

BROOKLYN HUSTLAZ

By **Boogsy Morina**

BROOKLYN ON LOCK I & II

By **Sonovia**

GANGSTA CITY

By **Teddy Duke**

A DRUG KING AND HIS DIAMOND I & II III

A DOPEMAN'S RICHES

HER MAN, MINE'S TOO I, II

CASH MONEY HO'S

By **Nicole Goosby**

TRAPHOUSE KING **I II & III**

KINGPIN KILLAZ I II III

STREET KINGS I II

PAID IN BLOOD
By **Hood Rich**
LIPSTICK KILLAH **I, II, III**
CRIME OF PASSION I & II
By **Mimi**
STEADY MOBBN' **I, II, III**
By **Marcellus Allen**
WHO SHOT YA **I, II, III**
Renta
GORILLAZ IN THE BAY **I II III**
DE'KARI
TRIGGADALE I II
Elijah R. Freeman
GOD BLESS THE TRAPPERS I, II, III
THESE SCANDALOUS STREETS I, II, III
FEAR MY GANGSTA I, II, III
THESE STREETS DON'T LOVE NOBODY I, II
BURY ME A G I, II, III, IV, V
A GANGSTA'S EMPIRE I, II, III, IV
THE DOPEMAN'S BODYGAURD
Tranay Adams
THE STREETS ARE CALLING
Duquie Wilson
MARRIED TO A BOSS... I II
By Destiny Skai & Chris Green
KINGZ OF THE GAME I II III
Playa Ray

SLAUGHTER GANG I II
By Willie Slaughter
THE HEART OF A SAVAGE
By Jibril Williams
FUK SHYT
By Blakk Diamond

BOOKS BY LDP'S CEO, CA$H

TRUST IN NO MAN

TRUST IN NO MAN 2

TRUST IN NO MAN 3

BONDED BY BLOOD

SHORTY GOT A THUG

THUGS CRY

THUGS CRY 2

THUGS CRY 3

TRUST NO BITCH

TRUST NO BITCH 2

TRUST NO BITCH 3

TIL MY CASKET DROPS

RESTRAINING ORDER

RESTRAINING ORDER 2

IN LOVE WITH A CONVICT

Coming Soon

BONDED BY BLOOD 2

BOW DOWN TO MY GANGSTA

Street Kings 2

www.ingramcontent.com/pod-product-compliance
Lightning Source LLC
Chambersburg PA
CBHW070511260626
47161CB00004B/1522